+
Sp465w

ACKNOWLEDGMENTS:
Thanks to Beverly McGlamry for her encouragement
and Harriet Abels for her help.

For Milt McAuley,
my hiking leader, who first brought me
into the land of the Chumash

WHITE HARE'S HORSES

Penina Keen Spinka

ATHENEUM   1991   NEW YORK

COLLIER MACMILLAN CANADA
Toronto

MAXWELL MACMILLAN INTERNATIONAL PUBLISHING GROUP
New York   Oxford   Singapore   Sydney

Atheneum
Macmillan Publishing Company
866 Third Avenue
New York, NY 10022

Collier Macmillan Canada, Inc.
1200 Eglinton Avenue East
Suite 200
Don Mills, Ontario M3C 3N1

First edition
Printed in the United States of America
Designed by Anne Scatto
1 2 3 4 5 6 7 8 9 10

Library of Congress Cataloging-in-Publication Data
Spinka, Penina Keen.
White Hare's horses / Penina Keen Spinka.
p. cm.
Summary: In sixteenth-century California, a young Chumash Indian, White Hare, must find the courage to save her people from Aztec invaders with their frightening horses.
ISBN 0–689–31654–2
1. Chumashan Indians—Juvenile fiction. [1. Chumashan Indians—Fiction. 2. Indians of North America—Fiction. 3. Aztecs—Fiction. 4. Horses—Fiction. 5. California—History—To 1846—Fiction.] I. Title.
PZ7.S75666Wh 1991
[Fic]—dc20

Contents

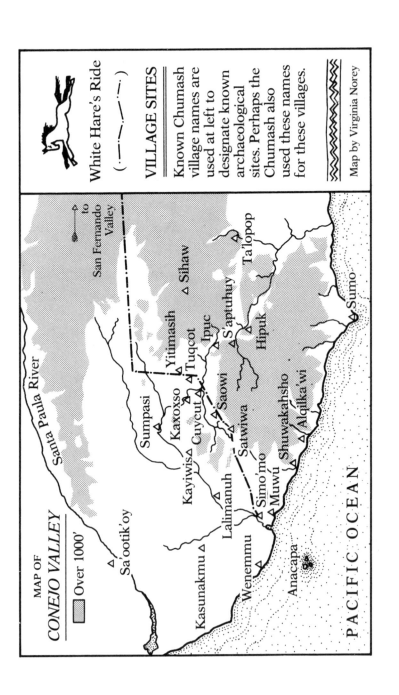

MAP OF
CONEJO VALLEY

□ Over 1000'

Santa Paula River

Sa'ootik'oy △

Sumpasi △

Kayiwis △

Kasunakmu △

Lalimanuh △

Wenemmu

Simo'mo △
Muwu △

PACIFIC OCEAN

Anacapa

Kaxoxso △
Cuycut △
Satwiwa

Shuwakahsho

Saowi △

Yitimasih
Tuqcot △
Ipuc

S'aptuhuy △

Hipuk

Alqilka'wi △

Ta'lopop

Sihaw △

Sumo △

to
San Fernando
Valley

White Hare's Ride
(· — · · — ·)

VILLAGE SITES

Known Chumash
village names are
used at left to
designate known
archaeological
sites. Perhaps the
Chumash also
used these names
for these villages.

Map by Virginia Norey

Grandfather

White Hare knew something was wrong when she saw her mother, Blue Star, running up the hill toward the meadow where she and her friends were digging for roots. She dropped her digging stick and ran toward her.

"Your grandfather," Mother gasped, waiting for a moment to catch her breath so she could speak. Mother's black hair was mixed with gray, and she could no longer run the trails as she once did. "He's dying!" she said. "Strong Arm found him in the woods where he went to gather firewood. He carried him to the ceremony cave and ran to the village for help. A priestess went to attend him. I ran for you."

"Grandfather shouldn't be at the cave; he should be in the siliak." The girl tried to gather her thoughts. Usually, those injured or suddenly taken ill were brought to the ceremonial enclosure within the village. But Grandfather couldn't be dying. He was not even sick.

He'd spoken to her this morning when she and the

others were leaving for the meadow, her gathering basket resting lightly on her back and secured by a woven
grass band to the basket hat she wore. "Come back
with it full, my little rabbit," he'd told her. His face
creased with the special smile he used for his only
grandchild. "I'm hungry for wild carrots."

She'd made sure to find a bunch for him. Now he
would never eat them. Had something struck him
down? How could he be dying? White Hare looked to
her mother for an explanation.

Mother's eyes closed for a moment. "My father is too
weak to be moved so far now. He can no longer speak
so we don't know how it happened, but there is no
mark on him. Sometimes, a sickness comes on all at
once. It is not for us to question the ways of the
Mother."

The Mother was the force all around them, the force
of life and nature; the earth herself. If she chose to take
Grandfather now, there was nothing to do and no med-
icine or prayer that could make him well again.

"I'm certain he will want to see you before his spirit
leaves him, if the Mother will give him time. He loves
you very much."

White Hare put her arms around her mother at once.
The older woman stroked her hair. It was as if a dark
cloud came over the sun. The other gatherers looked
away to give them privacy.

"Do you remember the way to the cave?"

"Yes, Mama." It did not seem possible. Grandfather
was like one of the mountains to her. She could no
more imagine him gone than one of them. Her other
grandfather had died before she was born, lost in a
storm on a trading visit to one of the island villages.

He was washed overboard from the large planked canoe by a big wave and the others could not even bring home his body for burial. Both grandmothers joined the spirit world before White Hare's seventh summer.

"Run quickly, then. I'll bring in your basket," Mother said.

White Hare felt the tears begin as she ran toward the cave. She shook her head fiercely to clear her eyes.

Grandfather's own bed furs were brought to make him comfortable, and a fire burned nearby. He was covered with his own rabbit robe. An antap priestess was already saying prayers for the ease of his journey. She did not stop her chanting even when she saw White Hare standing in the entrance of the cave.

The priestess held out an abalone shell with burning white sage leaves to the four holy directions: east for beginnings, west for endings, north and south for the two holy mountains. Then she blew the smoke over Grandfather to purify his spirit for its journey. The pungent smell filled the air, making White Hare cough. The priestess motioned for her to come closer.

The girl had never before been so close to someone who was dying. It pained her to see her grandfather's heavily lidded eyes only half opened, with the whites showing. She felt a shiver in spite of the fire's warmth. Every little while, Grandfather's chest rose and fell as his body struggled to take another breath.

White Hare looked toward the priestess. Her face was painted white with black stripes under her chin in the traditional antap paint. She was a doctor, skilled in healing as well. She knew herbs and setting bones and sewing skin, and so she had saved many lives.

White Hare knew the priestess could see things that were beyond her own range of vision.

"Oh," the priestess said in the same singsong tone she used for the prayers. "I feel the spirits are gathering. They are getting ready to receive him. It will be tonight."

"Is he hurting?" White Hare asked.

"He is beyond that," the priestess replied. "Move closer to him. His thoughts are reaching out to you."

White Hare lowered herself closer to her grandfather's head. She stroked his gray hair. Then she leaned forward to kiss his grizzled cheek. "Grandfather," she whispered. "I'm here. It's White Hare." She did not know if his ears heard her voice, but if he was here, still in this body before her, he heard her thoughts. She took his hand and listened for an answer.

Grandfather's voice sounded only in her head, yet was stronger than she remembered ever hearing it before. She closed her eyes and listened hard.

"You are still young, my little rabbit. You are afraid because I am dying. Do not be afraid and do not be angry. The Mother is with me, and she is giving me an easy departure. She has waited so I could tell you good-bye, so you see, she is very kind. You must try to stop being afraid so easily. You will need your courage some day."

"What do you mean, Grandfather?" Her lips made the words, even though she did not speak aloud. Her hand rested on Grandfather's forehead.

"You are Chupu's child, a child of nature, of Mother Earth. The Powers will answer you when you need them." In her head, White Hare felt his smile and a wink. She understood that he was trying to reassure her about his death, but it seemed there was something more.

Grandfather's voice continued to speak to her. "Our mountains are not the whole world. There are foreign places and strange people who can cross vast distances. I have seen strangers in dreams. They are real. You will see, one day."

"But I don't want to go to faraway places. This is where my home is." White Hare felt certain her grandfather was not trying to frighten her. He was trying to warn her, though. She knew she should be grateful, but his words gave her a chill.

"Your love and your courage may be needed to save our home. If you have need of guidance, I will hear you at the reflecting waters. Now grow and be happy. Develop your strengths. I will speak to your mother."

White Hare looked around. Her mother stood close by. She backed away to allow Blue Star to come closer. Then she ran from the cave. Her father was still out hunting, so their keesh would be empty. She could be alone.

Long Eye, her best friend, stepped up to her as her path brought her near the midden. Long Eye carried a burden basket filled with shells and debris from her family's keesh. A death in the village was a reason for cleaning house.

"Would you like me to be with you now?" her friend asked, hesitantly. "Emptying this won't take very long." When White Hare hesitated, she added hastily. "I understand if you want to be alone."

White Hare kissed Long Eye's cheek. "I really do want to be by myself just now. Thank you for understanding. Maybe tomorrow, I will come to your keesh for a while." Long Eye looked after her sadly as White Hare continued down the path to the village.

White Hare's keesh was a sturdily built home, and its strength welcomed her. It was constructed, with sycamore posts bound into a circle and wrapped around with supple young willow branches. Tule reeds were neatly woven between the willow branches. The thatching repelled water and made it drip away from the interior even during the winter storms. It was dim inside even on this sunny day, since the only light came from the smoke hole and the small entrance. White Hare pulled a woven rush mat to cover the door.

Her bed was an antelope skin stretched over a wooden frame built into the wall. It was covered with soft grasses and furs, and she lay on it to ponder Grandfather's last words to her.

"What did Grandfather mean?" she wondered. Be happy. Have courage. Grow. Save the home of the People. Strangers and faraway places. The words spun in her head and she could make no sense of them. Perhaps, someday, they would become clear. She covered herself with the robe on her bed, adjusting it to block out light from the smoke hole. She wanted to be completely alone with her thoughts and feelings.

White Hare lay with her face to the Earth, Earth who would soon accept Grandfather into herself as she had taken White Hare's ancestors from these mountain villages for uncountable years.

Grandfather was not antap, but he was well respected in the village for his practical wisdom. When a villager asked him for advice, often he paused. It was assumed the powers spoke to him. He said they would speak to her also, if she needed them. Speaking to unseen powers might be frightening. Grandfather told her to stop being frightened so easily. She wondered if it was possible to face the unknown without fear. Tears started again when she heard the death wails begin. This time, she did not shake the tears away.

She must have slept, for when her father, Goat Killer, entered the keesh, it was almost dark. He carried a goat over his shoulder, a small one, but the meat would be welcome.

"White Hare," he said softly. "Are you awake?"

"Yes, Father. Do you know about Grandfather?"

"I saw your mother at the cave. She'll stay with him tonight. He was always a good father-in-law to me. He was the first, beside your mother, to welcome me to Simo'mo. My heart is heavy with his loss. Do you want to sit with your mother? I can carve up the goat myself and hang it over the smoke fire."

"Thank you, Father." His hands were still dusty and stained from the hunt, but she pressed close to him and felt his warmth before she went out into the dark.

"Only eleven summers," she heard him murmur from just outside. "It won't be long before she is happy again."

She was not happy when she and her mother followed Grandfather to the cemetery near the village for burial, nor when her long hair was cut close to the scalp to indicate her state of mourning. She was not happy when she put the ashes on her face.

In spite of the death of an important person, food gathering was not put off for very long. When a group of young people set off down the trail to the beach, White Hare was with them, her carrying basket on her back.

The girls dug in the sand or scraped mussels off the rocks. Out over the water, between the large plank canoes called tomols, the boys spread their nets.

"That's enough," the oldest girl said, clapping her hands to rid them of sand. "The baskets are filled." She and a few other of the oldest directed them to place the baskets out of the sun and cover them with seaweed. "Let's clean off."

White Hare dove into the waves. The water was warm. She swam strongly and soon left the others behind, playing in the surf. She could see Anacapa shining green in the sun. There were other islands farther out. Someday, she thought, she might like to see them and visit the villages there.

She knew Chumash land extended north for a long way, perhaps a month's travel. There were big villages, towns, where fine tools were made and the greatboats, too. Once, when she visited Muwu she had even seen a strange thing called pottery. She traded some blue shell money for a piece of it to bring to her mother. Blue Star looked it over. It was too breakable to use, she concluded, but it was fine to put flowers in. Tightly woven, waterproof baskets were best for carrying and cooking, and shells made the best plates and bowls. Also, they did not cost anything.

White Hare wondered as she swam if one of the islands, or a big Chumash town, was what Grandfather meant when he spoke of faraway places. On the other side of the mountains, there was a huge valley and then the desert. Not many people lived there. After the islands, the ocean went on forever.

Her strong kicks brought her halfway to the tomols.

She waved to the boys on board, and they returned her greetings. At last, she turned for shore.

White Hare ran out of the waves, shaking her close-cut hair like a dog to get rid of the water. She was used to the weight of waist-length hair clinging to the water. She felt light enough now to rise into the air. Her grass sandals were in the shade where she had left them to protect her feet from the hot sand. She rubbed her feet dry and put the sandals on. She carried her short reed skirt while the wind blew her dry until she came up to the hill where the long grasses grew and the other maidens were resting after their swim.

She picked a place next to Long Eye and settled herself down to rest and finish drying in the warm sun. There was enough food in the baskets to keep the village happy and full for days. It felt so good to be clean and to let the sun bathe her body with warmth. She closed her eyes and smiled a contented smile.

Long Eye moved beside her and touched her softly. "The boys are gathering in the nets." White Hare propped herself up on one elbow to look at her. Her friend's pretty mouth was turned down in an unhappy pout.

"You know we have to get back before the sun goes to bed," White Hare sighed. It felt so good to lie and do nothing. "I wish we could stay here tonight and go home tomorrow, but the women have to cook the food before it all goes bad. Are you sad because we have to go?"

"Yes," Long Eye agreed. "I wish I could stay here forever. I sometimes wish I could be one of the crabs walking on the sand so I wouldn't have to leave at all. It's so pretty on the beach."

"You wouldn't feel that way if you were caught in a storm," White Hare reminded her. "Besides, a seabird would swoop down and swallow you in one bite, and then who would I have to tell my secrets to?" White Hare smiled and sat up. "You sit up too. I'll plait your hair." She combed Long Eyes's hair with her fingers. It was beginning to wave slightly as it dried, and White Hare was already deciding which of the many flowers growing nearby she would weave into her friend's hair to beautify her. She rose to gather some.

Long Eye had her shell necklace hanging low between her small breasts. The name suited her, because she was usually the first to see anything. In her fourth year, she pointed out the men who were returning from a ten-day trading visit to some of the northern villages. They traded for furs and bone arrow tips and the small nuts found inside the cones in the pine forests to the north. Her family named her Long Eye on the spot to replace her baby name.

White Hare thought she should have been given a name to do with the sea. Perhaps, when the time came for her to wed, she would change her name again. White Hare was given her own name because she startled easily and ran quickly, usually when she was frightened. It suited now, but someday, White Hare knew she would have another name. She wondered sometimes what it would be.

Before long, she had a handful of the pretty golden flowers that grew singly along the side of the trail and she was back. "You will smell as lovely as you look," she told Long Eye as she worked the stems into her braids. "There. One behind each ear as well." She tucked them in. "If I were Dancing Bear, I would want to sleep with you tonight. I saw how he looked at you from his tomol. You're almost old enough to choose your husband and then I will have your baby to play with."

"You're less than two years behind me, and I haven't seen thirteen summers yet. Don't push me so hard to pair off. I'm in no hurry to tend a baby. Besides, I think it was you Dancing Bear was looking at. Now I know why you want to make me so pretty. Your hair is unusual because it's short now; I think all the boys are looking at you. I saw some white flowers growing up the hill a little way. You can make your own baby if you want one to play with. I want to keep coming down to the shore. You can sit with the old women and pound acorns and listen to the babies cry if you want to."

White Hare laughed as Long Eye moved up the hill behind them. "I'm too little to make a baby yet." She pointed to her breasts, which had hardly begun to grow.

"Besides, you run too fast," her friend pointed out. "One of the young men would have to catch you first."

When they joined the others by the filled baskets, White Hare seemed to have white stars in her hair, and Dancing Bear with his baskets of fish hanging down from his shoulders was indeed smiling to her.

She questioned, only for a moment, if it was right to feel happy again as soon as father said she would. Then she remembered. Grandfather had told her to be happy. She was young. Her friends were with her and the mountains were beautiful and the flowers in bloom as the gathering band wended their way up the trail until they were far above the ocean. It was good to be happy, she realized, and wrong to resist it. But still, she knew she would never forget her grandfather.

A Wedding Trip

Two years passed. White Hare was twelve now. A special wedding ceremony was to take place between White Hare's village of Simo'mo and the village of Satwiwa. Since weddings between important people were almost as much fun as Solstice Day celebrations, White Hare looked forward to going to the neighboring village with excitement.

Half of White Hare's village rose early to begin the trek on the day of the wedding feast between the wot of Satwiwa and an antap maiden of Simo'mo. Satwiwa was half a day's journey away.

White Hare walked along with her parents for a while. She was wearing her newest skirt. On her shoulders she carried her bedroll and gifts for her cousins, who lived in the village under the bluffs.

"Run along, White Hare." Blue Star smiled at her daughter. "I can see we're going too slow for you."

White Hare took off, catching up with those in the lead a few minutes later. "There you are," Dancing Bear said. A few of the faster boys were walking together.

They paused on a high ridge to look at the view. Behind them, far in the distance, was the ocean. The islands were visable, but their villages were not. They were hidden in the mists. The sky was pale, not the intense blue of summer, and the leaves on some of the trees were changing to red and gold. A condor floated lazily above them. The people behind them colored the trail for a long way.

Although it was far, they could see down into the farther of the small valleys, possibly into Satwiwa itself. If that was the valley they saw, then the village was closed in by the bluffs. The next part of the trail was downhill. By now White Hare had her breath under control. "I'll race you to the top of the next hill," she challenged.

"Who?" four voices inquired.

"Anyone who wants to. Come on. Don't be slow-pokes." She was off, with Dancing Bear right behind her. Wolf and Hawk decided to join the race. The older boys went another way, looking for some game, deer or rabbit, to bring to their hosts. White Hare was tall for twelve and the twelve-year-old boys had not yet reached their full height, so it was a fair match.

White Hare and Dancing Bear soon outdistanced the others. They stopped when they got to the next ridge, breathing hard. "Well, who won?" Dancing Bear took a sip of water from the skin he carried on his belt. He offered her a swallow.

"We did. We're way ahead of everyone."

They were the first to see the inland village. It was neatly set out between a pond and the huge bluffs for which Satwiwa was named. While the others set up camp, Dancing Bear and White Hare went exploring.

A trail led to a waterfall White Hare remembered seeing the last time she was here. The water ran strongly then, falling in several levels and making pools. Maple trees grew near the banks in the shade. The rocks at the edge of the pool were covered with limestone deposits that the water left behind. The moss at the edge was cool on White Hare's toes. The fall was little more than a trickle now in the dry season, but White Hare stripped off her skirt and washed as well as she was able so she would be fresh for the dancing later.

"You could use a bath too," she said as she waited for the wind to dry her. She held her grass skirt in her hand. "Why don't you get in?"

"I'll go to the sweathouse later," Dancing Bear said, turning away so that White Hare could not see him. "I need to help my parents." He walked away quickly, not waiting for her.

She wondered if she had done something to offend him as she strolled toward the village. She tied her skirt around her waist and lifted her pack to her shoulders again. She had not gloated about beating him in the race, pretending they arrived at the summit together. Well, if he was going to be a sore loser . . . He did not seem upset until she stood under the water, though. Boys were strange sometimes, she decided.

In the village, she found the keesh of her aunt and uncle and her young cousins. She greeted them with hugs and set down her pack to give them their gifts. The elders eagerly swallowed the smoked shellfish she handed them. They did not get such treats every day. Then she gave the little baskets she had been working on for a month to her cousins. She had gathered the pine needles herself and constructed them under her mother's masterly supervision. She was pleased with the way they turned out. Her cousins admired them.

"Aunt Blue Star and Uncle Goat Killer were here already," Bobcat told her, indicating the sleeping rolls. "They went to the sweathouses. Leave your roll here. Fern and I want to show you the village. It's grown since the last time you were here."

Bobcat took her outside. Little Fern came along, holding her new basket in one hand and her cousin's in the other. "Did you see the cactus patch?" Bobcat asked. "I'll wager you didn't see one fruit. We got them all and they're soaking now so the prickers don't get in our fingers and we won't have to hold them on sticks either."

"You talk a lot." White Hare laughed as she and nine-year-old Bobcat and five-year-old little Fern made their way through the streets of the village. It was always fun to see them.

The sun went behind the hill, and the air began to cool. Some of the people walking by were carrying woven rush mats and baskets of food for the party; many of them already wore their evening robes. White Hare was thinking about going back for her sleeping robe to throw over her shoulders when she passed something she had never seen before. She opened her eyes wide at the strange sight.

Within a small keesh-like structure, but without its overlay of tule reeds, were a family or two of rabbits. They scampered about on the inside, wiggling their noses and gnawing at the roots and grasses lying on the ground.

"Why are they in there?" White Hare asked curiously.

She bent down and patted one of the young ones who lay close to the edge. "Is it a trap?"

"No," Bobcat explained, full of importance at knowing something his big cousin did not. "It's called a hutch. The rabbits breed and we can just pull one out and kill it whenever we're hungry for rabbit. We don't have to catch one. Isn't that clever?"

"I don't think it's fair," White Hare responded, frowning. "You feed them and they think you're their friend. Then you just reach in and kill one. That's cruel."

"Oh, you're just saying that because your name is White Hare, so you don't like to see rabbits killed."

"How would you like to see someone eat a bobcat, Bobcat?"

White Hare could not stop thinking about the poor rabbits as they walked on. Homes were decorated for the wedding as if for summer solstice, but with colored leaves and feathers instead of flowers.

The sound of laughter caused White Hare and her cousins to turn and look back. Some boys were pushing long, pointed sticks through the openings in the hutch. The animals were hopping toward the other side where more boys were waiting with sticks.

"Let's go," Bobcat said. "I showed you the rabbits already."

White Hare was rooted to the ground. Her cheeks were flushed and she took short, shallow breaths.

"Make them stop!" she hissed.

"Don't get so excited. It's only food." Bobcat sounded embarrassed. He grabbed her hand and tried to take her away.

"Only food!" she shouted, pulling her hand out of

his grasp. "They have feelings!" She was back at the hutch in a moment.

"Get away from them. Leave them alone!" White Hare was shaking in her rage. The boys pulled back in shock. She was bigger than they were. A moment later, however, their leader challenged her. There were five of them and only one of her.

"Who are you to tell us what to do?"

White Hare swallowed. Her rage had pushed her this far, but it was not fazing these boys. What was she going to do now? She had not thought this far ahead and had made no plan. They glared at her, daring her to oppose them further. Her first impulse was to run, but if she did, who would defend the poor rabbits? Food was one thing. Torture was another.

"I'm White Hare of Simo'mo, and I won't let you hurt these animals."

"White Hare!" the leader said derisively. "She's nothing but a rabbit herself. What are you going to do about it, rabbit?" He picked up his stick again and pretended to poke it at one of the rabbit mothers, who was actually in the middle of the hutch, not in poking distance.

"*This!*" White Hare pushed the leader hard and while he sprawled in the dust with the others staring incredulously, she tore the posts of the hutch out of the ground and scattered the rabbits, which were soon no more than specks in the distance. As they all watched, the rabbits disappeared into the cactus patch that covered half of the nearby hillside.

The boys ran, leaving White Hare standing there with Bobcat and Little Fern. "What did you do, Cousin

White Hare?" Fern asked. To her, the whole thing was a game. She could not understand the look of horror on her cousin's face.

"You're going to be in trouble," Bobcat said seriously. "Those rabbits belonged to someone. No! Wait! Come back!"

Before he could stop her, White Hare was halfway to the cactus patch herself.

Justice

The wide sky above the mountain turned pink, then purple, then dusky blue as the stars came out. The moonlight made the grass look white. In the meadow above the bluffs White Hare sat, knees pressed to her chest, shivering. She wore only her milkweed fiber skirt. The wind rattled the leaves in a nearby sycamore tree and she thought she heard the howl of a coyote farther up on the mountain.

"I act before I think," White Hare said aloud. "Will I ever learn? The wedding must be starting and I'm freezing. What am I going to do?"

"Go back, I think," said a voice behind her. She turned, startled. It was Dancing Bear.

"How did you know I was here?" She wiped her eyes.

"I guessed." Dancing Bear smiled.

"You should be at the wedding. Everybody will be looking for you," White Hare said. Her arms were around her body, and she shook with the cold as a new breeze stirred the grasses and leaves into small circles. Her teeth chattered.

"Listen to who's talking. Here. Put this on." He put his robe around her. "Let's get back. Your parents are getting worried."

"But I let the rabbits get away. They belonged to somebody. I can't go back. I don't know what they'll do to me."

"There will probably be a trial or something tomorrow. The wot of the village will decide what your punishment will be."

White Hare gasped, her eyes widening.

"He'll probably punish the boys too," Dancing Bear said consolingly. "Yes, I heard the whole story from your cousin. I knew you were with him. Let's get back now. There's no reason to miss the wedding."

The moon was moving higher in the sky. The wot of the village and his bride stood in the middle of the holy circle. With the twelve consecrated antap in their places around the circle and Satwiwa's alchuklash, who was both astrologer and high priest, standing opposite the couple, the ceremony began.

The alchuklash led the chanting. He invoked Chupu, the Earth Mother, to witness this joining of people. He asked for her blessings that the marriage be successful and fertile.

"May Satwiwa and Simo'mo be joined always in friendship and kindness as these two are joined in the sight of the Mother," he intoned.

"May it be a blessing for all of us," the lower priests responded.

"May it be her will," the common people of both villages sang together. Everyone rushed to congratulate the newly wedded pair and each other. Blue Star and Goat Killer hung back from the happy commotion, however. They had their eyes on the road. Blue Star saw White Hare first and rushed to embrace her daughter tearfully.

"My child," she murmured. "I thought you were lost to us. Don't you know wolves prowl the mountains and lions hunt at night?"

"I'm sorry for worrying you," White Hare stammered. She knew, but again, she had not thought.

"Thank you for bringing her back to us, Dancing Bear. Come." Her father took her by the hand. "Let's get you something to eat. Have you eaten yet, Dancing Bear?"

"Oh, yes, I have eaten." He backed away to leave the family to itself, wondering if he could find his own mother and father in this crowd. They had no cousins to spend the night with, and he had to make sure they had their site picked out and were comfortable.

White Hare found Long Eye when the dancing began. "Where were you all day?" White Hare asked her friend as they joined hands and began the stately turns of the early dancing.

"Oh, here and there. I made a new friend." Long Eye looked lovely as usual. She was shorter than White Hare and more womanly. She had just seen her fourteenth summer. Her hips were rounded; her breasts bounced in the firelight as she swayed and jumped. "I hear you had quite an adventure."

White Hare felt her face grow hot, even hotter than her body had grown from the dancing. She no longer felt the need for Dancing Bear's robe.

"My adventure was nothing but trouble," White Hare

said briefly. "I don't want to think about it right now. I'm sure someone will remind me tomorrow. Tell me about your new friend."

"Well, he's tall and he's good-looking and he's coming over to us right now." A young man was swiftly approaching them. The firelight reflected in his eyes. White Hare was shocked to see Long Eye looking at him in a way that was both inviting and something else, as if she had special, secret plans for him.

"When Long Eye told me she had made a new friend, I thought she meant a girl," White Hare blurted out and then put her hand over her mouth.

"Red Antler, I'd like you to meet my best friend, White Hare," Long Eye said graciously.

"I am happy to meet you, White Hare," Red Antler said laughing. "So you're the White Hare everyone is talking about."

Waves of heat washed over her again. Oh no, White Hare thought. The whole world knows what I did.

"I hope you won't mind finding another partner," Red Antler said, taking Long Eye's hand in his. "Your friend and I have only met recently, and we would like to get to know each other better."

Long Eye only murmured something about seeing her tomorrow as she let him lead her away. She didn't even tell him she'd rather be with me, White Hare thought bitterly. She looked around her. Other people were caught in the spirit of the day. She let the music take her again and began to sway and move her feet with the sound. She took the hand of the closest free maiden and danced fiercely with her, trying to crowd out her confused emotions. The girl tired, so White Hare looked for another who could keep up with her.

When the second maiden excused herself, White Hare found she was perspiring, but only beginning to feel calm again.

She looked for a third partner when Dancing Bear stepped up to her. "This is yours," she said, removing the robe. She had been afraid to lay it down for fear it would get lost.

He put it over his shoulders. "Dance with me," he said simply. The drums and the flutes played slower now, and there were fewer dancers. She did not see Long Eye anywhere. Her cousins had been put to bed long before. Even her aunt and uncle and her parents were gone. The musicians would play as long as there were dancers. There were several drummers and flutists who took turns.

Dancing Bear took her by the hand and led her from the dance floor. She thought at first that he was taking her back to the home of her relatives. She felt slightly dizzy and disoriented from the dancing, so she did not realize where they were going until she found herself in a wooded area away from the homes.

Small cries and sighs rose from the ground as they passed couples embracing under the trees. She knew this was acceptable, in fact, many marriages were arranged between young couples who had gotten to know each other this way during holidays and social gatherings. Weddings led to more weddings, was the saying. Still, she knew this was not for her. Not now and not like this. She could not think of the right words to say. She and Dancing Bear were friends. They ran together and played together. She tried to gather her thoughts.

At last he stopped. Her back was against a tree. They were only a little off the trail. There were soft grasses and leaves underfoot. Finally, she found her voice. "I'm your friend, Dancing Bear. We aren't supposed to be together like this."

"Who said we aren't?" Dancing Bear seemed to know what he wanted. His sureness left her feeling more confused about the best way to handle this.

"I'm too young anyway. You know that. Aren't you too young for that kind of thing, too? We're both the same age."

"Some boys grow up fast." His voice became harsher. If she did not get away from him soon, she knew she would regret it and eventually, so would he.

"If you're my friend, don't do this," White Hare protested.

She had no space behind her to back up. Dancing Bear came forward and put his hands to her shoulder to draw her closer. She tried to duck, but he held her fast and he was the stronger. She was slender, but he was stocky and muscular. It could not be a battle of strength. She had to make him understand how she felt.

She began to shake as his arms came around her. He let go of her abruptly, but he did not step aside.

"You're not a hunter and I'm not a deer. Don't corner me," she said.

"No," he answered. His voice deepened. "I'm not a hunter. I'm a fisherman, and there are plenty of other fish in the ocean. I'll find someone else." He spun on his heel and walked swiftly away from her.

She walked slowly back to the keesh of her aunt and uncle. Dancing Bear's behavior had distressed her. Perhaps he wanted to make himself feel older by taking a maiden. But to her, they were still children. It must be the music and the influence of seeing the others. When he found her in the meadow, he was himself. Tonight and this afternoon, by the waterfall, he had been like a stranger she did not understand.

She heard her parents sigh in relief as she came into the keesh in the dark. She found her sleeping roll where she left it. Thinking about Dancing Bear was getting her nowhere. Soon she was covered with her robe and fast asleep. It was the rabbits she dreamed about that night. Her trial was yet to come.

Even though it was the day after his wedding, the wot of Satwiwa heard her case the next day in the council hut, the siliak. He sat cross-legged on his mat to listen and give judgment. Even though he was young and not long in his office, he was considered wise. In village disputes, even the antap could not question his decisions.

White Hare's cousin Bobcat was allowed to testify first. He swallowed his words and had to be told to speak up so all could hear. The boys told their side of the story without embarrassment. They felt a guest had no right to interfere with their fun.

Then the owner of the rabbit hutch talked about how long it had taken him to make it, and how long to catch the rabbits. This was an experiment that might have benefited the entire village, he said.

White Hare listened with her head hanging down. She had brought shame to her parents and to Simo'mo. All eyes were on her now as the wot turned to her. She wanted to crawl away and hide, but that would shame her parents further. She kept her back straight and waited, accepting in advance whatever punishment he would speak. With the acceptance, her fear decreased, but only slightly. At least she could compose herself so that it would not show.

"What do you have to say in your defense?" the wot asked White Hare gently. Her hand rose to her mouth in surprise. She lowered it and stood with her hands to her sides again as she thought and searched for words.

It was difficult for her to know how to tell her story. Bobcat had told exactly what she did and what the boys did. The only thing that could be added was how she felt. She closed her eyes for a moment, bringing back to her mind how the laughing boys poked the defenseless rabbits. Then, the words came pouring out.

"The poor animals were all caged up, and they couldn't run or fight back. The boys were hurting them with sharp sticks. It wasn't fair. Even if the rabbits must be food to eat, they are alive now. They aren't toys to poke. They can feel. Those boys were hurting the babies right in front of their mothers." White Hare was shocked at herself for speaking so much. It was not like her, but now she could not help it. She felt again the rage that possessed her yesterday at the mistreatment of things that could not defend themselves.

Still, she knew she had done wrong. "I am sorry," she said to the owner of the hutch.

"I think I understand how it happened now," the wot said from his mat. "This is my decision. White Hare will stay in Satwiwa until she can repair the hutch and help to catch alive one female and one male rabbit."

The boys snickered at this. White Hare's family looked grim.

"I'll take her back across the mountains when she's

completed the task," White Hare's uncle whispered to her parents.

"And you, Spotted Toad," the wot continued to the leader of the boys, "and you," he said to each of them in turn, calling them by name in front of the combined village elders as he pronounced his decision, "will be taken home by your parents and given a sound beating with willow switches to make you understand the meaning of pain. If you are ever seen inflicting pain on a caged creature again, the lesson will need to be repeated. It was not very brave to torment caged rabbits. Let me hear that you were brave enough to take your punishment without complaint. I have done speaking. This trial is over."

There were nods and smiles from all around the assembled as the boys were led away.

It was now midmorning and time to make their farewells. The Simo'moans had more than half a day's journey before them. White Hare had never been away from her parents before. Her aunt and uncle would have to take their places until she earned the right to go home, but still, a tear slipped down her cheek as she embraced her parents before the doorway. She watched as her friends and family took their places in the long line of people. How long would it take, she wondered, to catch the rabbits?

Dancing Bear came up to her before he joined his parents. He hung his head. "I'm very sorry," he said hestitantly. He looked at the ground.

"The decision of the wot was fair," White Hare said.

"That's not what I mean. Please forgive me for the way I behaved last night after the dancing. I know it was wrong of me. I just hope we can be friends again.

I will really miss you until you come back." He sounded like he meant it. He truly was ashamed.

White Hare smiled at last. "Let's pretend last night never happened. We're friends again."

He returned her smile.

"But I may never get home again," she reminded him. "I have no idea how to catch rabbits. I may have to stay here forever."

Dancing Bear leaned forward and whispered something into her ear. When he moved back, she knew something she did not know before. It would take some figuring out, but it could work.

He took his place in the line. A wave, a concerned look from her mother and father, a smile to her friends before they turned their faces to the trail, and the long line began to move.

White Hare stood next to Little Fern and watched until all the people of her home village were gone. She felt a squeeze as the little girl's fingers slipped into hers. She looked down. Her cousin was smiling. "I'm going to pretend you're my big sister the whole time you stay with us. Is that all right?"

"Of course we can pretend. We can keep pretending even when I go home and you come to visit me. When you come, I'll teach you how to swim in the ocean. You'll be the best swimmer in all of Satwiwa and everyone will envy you."

Little Fern started to smile, then a dark look crossed her face. "You can't go home to Simo'mo yet. You know what the wot said. You have to live here until you catch two rabbits, a mama rabbit and a papa rabbit."

White Hare's aunt, who had gone back into her keesh, returned with her digging stick and a big basket on her back. Uncle was already gone with the hunters. "Girls," Aunt said, "I must go. We need more food. All our company had big appetites. White Hare, I know you're sad about being left behind. You can play with Little Fern and think about what you're going to do about those rabbits, but tomorrow you'll have to start working like the other girls your age. No one is allowed to be lazy here."

"We aren't lazy in Simo'mo either," White Hare said. She had to defend her village. "I know how to work hard. You'll see."

Aunt gave both of them a hug. She had on her broad-brimmed straw hat to shade her eyes. It also cushioned the heavy basket band around her forehead that held the burden basket. Other women joined her, soon they were out of sight. White Hare heard the sound of singing and pounding. The old women and the young mothers with babies were already breaking up more acorns and grinding them into meal for gruel and bread.

"What do you want to do today, Sister White Hare?" White Hare gathered Little Fern close to her and told her.

"First we'll fix the hutch. That will be the easy part. Then we'll get your friends. It will be our secret now, a girls' secret. We'll surprise those bad boys. Don't even tell Bobcat."

Soon the hutch was mended. White Hare and Little Fern stood back to admire their work. "Now let's go find your friends."

White Hare found sharp stones for all the small girls

by the time they were assembled. She walked with them to a spot of open ground away from trees or houses, where no one could spy on them.

"This is a special secret just for us girls," she told them after she explained what they were going to do. "Afterward, when they see how we did it, everyone will say how clever we were. Now are we all going to work together?"

"Yes," ten small voices answered. Their faces glowed with excitement.

"Are we going to be the best rabbit-catching team in all the mountains?"

"Yes!"

"Then let's go."

White Hare's troop spent the morning cutting long strands of autumn grass. The inland girls did not learn all the same skills White Hare was taught in her own village closer to the sea. She had to show them the knot-tying process several times and supervise the weaving of the grasses.

A few of the adults passed and watched the girls at work for a while before walking on.

Bobcat and some of his friends came by during the day. "What are you doing?" he asked, eyeing the knotted and woven work that was spreading out before the girls. Little Fern looked up fearfully.

"It's a game girls play in Simo'mo. Do you and your friends want to play too?" White Hare asked sweetly. "I can teach you—it's easy."

"Let's get out of here," one of the boys shouted. "Girls' games!" They laughed as they ran out of sight.

White Hare sent a few of the girls to bring back acorn bread and a basketful of water with a dipper for their lunch. They ate fast, then resumed their work.

When each girl had a good number of strands woven and knotted into loose squares, White Hare separated the girls into two groups of five. Each laid her square down next to the others and wove the ends together. Soon, with everyone working, they had two good strong nets. That was what Dancing Bear had whispered in her ear. "Nets. Use nets."

They picked up small stones as they walked to the cactus patch on the hill. Rabbits often hid there. The family White Hare released made straight for the hill. They knew it was a safe place to hide and make their homes. Coyotes and mountain cats could not follow them through the low cactus into their nests and warrens. Only a snake could catch a rabbit in a cactus patch.

Hunters sometimes stood with their bows and arrows ready while children threw rocks and yelled to scare the rabbits out. What made this different was that White Hare must catch the rabbits alive.

White Hare divided the girls one more time. Two groups of three carried each net upwind, so the breeze would not carry their scent to the creatures. She showed the girls how to hold the net and how to throw it. She was part of one of the groups of three. The rest of the girls stood downwind and waited for White Hare's signal.

"I hope we'll be lucky the first time," she whispered to the girls. "If it doesn't work, the rabbits might figure out what we're doing and stay in their houses. Or they'll watch for us and run the other way. We can never outrun them."

They got ready. White Hare made the motion of throwing a stone. The five girls at the far end suddenly raised their voices and pelted the thorny hiding place with their stones. They yelled as hard as they could, jumping in their excitement and reaching down for more stones to throw.

The rabbits broke out of their cover. The villagers were just in time to see the girls fling their nets over the first ones. White Hare hurried to tangle the rabbits up well within the net. She lifted the two her group caught. It took several of the smaller girls to lift the other bundle.

Half the village, including her aunt and uncle, Bobcat and the bigger boys, the wot and his new wife, were standing there to see five rabbits being handed to the owner of the rabbit hutch. White Hare barely had the time to say, "Girls, you were wonderful."

Their parents beamed with surprise and approval at what their young ones were able to accomplish.

White Hare walked alone to the wot of Satwiwa and smiled. "May I go home now?" she asked.

She felt as though she had grown since yesterday. The wot looked at her in a different way. "Of course," he said. "You taught our people something new today. Any time you wish to visit, you are welcome, but you may certainly go home. You've done even more than I required."

White Hare thanked him politely and went to stand by her aunt and uncle and Little Fern. "I told you, Aunt, we know how to work hard in Simo'mo."

Women's Matters

I t was spring. The world came to life again. Flowers bloomed in bright yellows and pinks and oranges on the mountain, and trees sprouted new leaves. Ponds and streams swelled with the winter rain. The rumble of the waterfall near Simo'mo was so loud that White Hare and Long Eye had to shout to make themselves heard beside it.

Each of them carried a small piece of soaproot in a pouch tied to her belt. The girls needed both hands to climb up the rocks to the small pool beneath the falls. A lone maple tree shaded the cascading water. It was one of their favorite places. Hot and sweaty from the climb, White Hair and Long Eye drank first. They hung their skirts over a low maple branch and stepped into the water.

They lathered up with wet soaproot, rubbed the foam over their bodies and into their hair. They splashed it off merrily as they enjoyed the water. After a while they climbed over to the rocks beside the falls to dry and talk.

"Red Antler is very handsome, don't you think?" Of course, it was Long Eye who spoke. She'd been starry-eyed ever since she met him last fall in Satwiwa, White Hare thought with displeasure. He had been here several times since then.

"You're not going to marry him and go away to live, are you? I'll never see you anymore." White Hare threw a pebble into the pool and watched it go over the lower falls. She was jealous of the attention Long Eye already gave the young man. Even when the two girls were alone, Long Eye wanted to talk about him.

"No," she answered, her mouth turning up in the corners. "He's coming here. He said he'd like to learn how to handle a tomol and fish with our men. We can build our home near yours. I'll still see you every day."

"You're really going to do it!" White Hare was astounded. She had been trying to make a joke. "How will we be friends? Your life will change when you're married. You'll be taking care of babies. When I come home from gathering, you'll want to be alone with him. I don't like this. Aren't you too young?"

Long Eye's hair was spread around her on the dry rocks. White Hare's which had grown only to her shoulders since the cutting when Grandfather died, was already half dry. The two girls had their legs spread out and were leaning back with their arms folded behind their heads.

"You know I'm not," Long Eye answered softly. White Hare could barely hear her over the water. "I've had to go to the menstrual hut six times already. I'm certainly old enough. Besides, Red Antler would be a friend to you too."

White Hare made a long face, not believing it. "Why are you in such a hurry to grow up?" she persisted. "You'll know when you feel that way about someone. You always wanted me to have babies so you could play with them. Don't you remember? Now I can do it. You didn't think I was going to do it alone, did you?" White Hare made another face at her friend. "I don't want to be with a man like that. Never. Well, not for a long time anyway. I'm going to stay young. I don't see why I should have to grow up until I'm good and ready." She dipped her feet into the water and kicked. "Just let me tell you," White Hare went on in a rush, "that you won't find *me* making eyes at the young men. I'm going to run and climb and swim and do all the things I like to do."

Long Eye sat up and shook her pretty head. Her hair brushed across the stones behind her. "You'll grow up when you're supposed to, just like I did. Come on. It's time to go home."

She stood up and reached for her skirt. When White Hare rose to follow her, Long Eye pointed back at the rock where White Hare had been sitting. "I think you're starting to grow up now, whether you want to or not."

White Hare looked back and saw where Long Eye pointed. There was blood on the stone. She shook her head angrily. "No. I don't want to have it. I'm too young." Tears began to well in her eyes and one slipped down her cheek. She brushed it away, but there were others behind it.

Long Eye looked into her friend's frightened young face. "It's not that bad, believe me. There are teas you can drink if it hurts at all. You're not hurting now, are you?"

"No." White Hare was ashamed of herself. Her mother told her this would happen to her, and she had no right to be making a fuss. Only her pride hurt her. She had just been bragging that she could control nature rather than the other way around. "The Mother made it happen now, to teach me a lesson, didn't she?"

"I don't think so," Long Eye said gently. "It would have happened anyway. We'll find some broad leaves and some cattail fluff or some dry moss near the stream on the way home. I'll show you what to do for now, but you need your mother. Come. Wash again first. In the menstrual hut, the antap women will give you instructions on everything you'll need to know. Don't go in. Just pretend the pool is a basket of water. That's fine. Now let's hurry."

White Hare sat unhappily in the special women's hut. She did not like to be away from the community. There were a few adults and a few of the maidens near her own age busy in the hut doing things that a woman in their condition was allowed to do. Tanning and sewing were allowed. Basket making and food preparation were not.

"This is a woman's matter," the antap priestess explained kindly to the new ones when she brought the women their meal. Her younger helper gave the women large shells to help themselves to the acorn mush and the clam stew. "Birth is a thing only a woman can understand. Except for the beginning, men have no part in it." Some of the older women tittered. Even White Hare smiled.

"Cast-off blood means no new life is beginning in

your womb. It is like a small death. This makes you vulnerable to jealous spirits who have no bodies and cannot make new life. Prayers will keep you safe, but you must not risk anyone else by being near them at this time." She went on to explain that baskets made now by them would rot and food prepared by them would be contaminated. Their very glance at a man could make a spirit angry, so men must not be near them. "You must see and keep company with women only until the blood ceases and you are purified in the women's sweathouse, our own temescal."

There's so much more to being a woman than I knew, White Hare thought sadly.

"Of course, when you're married," the priestess continued, "you'll be pregnant or nursing most of the time, so you won't be coming here very often. When you notice you are bleeding, you must always leave your children in another's care and leave the village immediately to come here."

"Sometimes it's a rest from all the chores," one of the older women said.

The priestess glared at her. Then she softened. "Well, maybe it is," she finally agreed. "But in any case, you must come here for the safety of your families and the entire village.

White Hare looked at her quizzically and shyly and then looked away, afraid to ask her question. She did not escape the notice of the priestess. "This is your first time, White Hare," the old woman said gently. "Tell me what is on your mind."

"It's just that I don't understand. Is it only humans who must be separated or do animals keep away from each other at this time? The dogs don't have their own hut, rabbits and goats and antelope don't isolate the females."

"Humans are more important than animals. The Mother has special rules for us to follow."

"But if a woman must leave the community, how can she ever be a good wot to her village?"

"A woman?" The priestess did not look amused although some of the others had their hands over their mouths to hide their smiles. A few of the younger girls giggled out loud.

"Yes," White Hare persisted. "I heard the story about the woman wot. Before she was born, the alchuklash told her mother the child would grow to unite three villages under one government. That was back in the days when there was war. Everyone expected the child to be a boy, a strong boy who would grow quickly to be their war leader and conquer the other two villages. Instead a girl was born and the alchuklash was ashamed and stepped down to let another take his place. The girl grew, and with great wisdom and peaceful ways, she fulfilled the prophecy. Now, how could such a thing happen when the girl had to leave the village five days out of every month?"

"She must have been old then, past the time for this," the priestess said. "Where did you hear the story about this woman? It is not one of the stories we tell."

"My mother's mother told me when I was very young," White Hare answered, "and I remember. The legend does not say she was an old woman."

"There you have it," the priestess said triumphantly. White Hare knew there was going to be a lecture. The old priestess loved to talk. "The story is only a legend.

We antap have guided the destinies of the Chumash for countless generations. The first people knew about the Earth Mother and the Sky People, but it was the antap who taught our people peace. We understand the months and the seasons and how to tell the passage of time by the stars. We predict the solstices. We know the difference between history and legends. You are a maiden of twelve summers. Do you want to challenge the wisdom of the antap? Do you think you could do a better job of teaching and leading our people? Do you long to become antap or perhaps even be a wot yourself?"

"No. No. I was only wondering." White Hare wished she had never spoken her mind. She had not meant to challenge anyone. The legend her grandmother once told her was one that stayed with her. She was thrilled at the thought of a woman leader. Of course, she herself would never aspire to such a place.

"Good," the priestess said. "You are a good girl. Don't wonder so much and don't ask so many questions. You'll be happier. Now, how would all of you like to hear some of the stories of long ago? I know stories of the adopted son of Datura and his adventures. I know stories of the Sun and his two daughters in their crystal house on the black side of the world and how they catch children and make skirts of their bones. I know about Scorpion Woman and the time Coyote went down beneath the sea to look for Eagle's nephew and was forced to live among the Swordfish People. I know of the days before people became people and all were animals."

The story telling went on until White Hare began to nod off. She curled up in her robe. Many of the women were still enjoying the stories and laughing. It was not bad to be here, White Hare realized, even though she could not agree with the purpose. Jealous evil spirits. It seemed to her that they were no more than another story to keep people entertained on the long winter nights. Challenging the antap was another matter. It was wiser to keep one's thoughts to oneself.

"You know," she whispered to a girl lying beside her, "I still like the story about the woman who became a wot."

"But she couldn't have when she was young," the girl said. "The antap woman said so."

"Maybe it was before the days when we had such silly rules," White Hare said, forgetting her resolve.

"Go to sleep," the other girl advised.

White Hare realized that she always questioned everything. She supposed it was one of her faults.

Strangers

The land was peaceful. The seasons came and went; spring and fall with their colors, the hot summers, and winter with its rainy days that turned the dry streambeds into rushing rivers for a little while.

White Hare was taller now, the tallest of the maidens. Her father said she grew as the spring grasses grew after the winter rains. Soon, her parents told her, it would be time to choose a young man for her husband. She made excuses. She was not ready to make her choice yet. In this, at least, she could delay.

She was a maiden of fifteen summers now, among the oldest to go down to the beach to harvest the clams and the mussels. Long Eye no longer came with them. She had changed her name to Pink Shell at her marriage. It was more appropriate. Red Antler, her doting husband, made her smile and blush when he whispered in her ear. White Hare had to smile whenever she thought about her friend's chubby twins. All the village became excited when Pink Shell gave birth to two healthy baby boys, Wiggler and Frog.

41

At the beach, White Hare was the first to see the strangely dressed man come around the bend in the land that sheltered their private cove. His nose and cheeks were much sharper than those of her people. She pointed and the others saw him. The boys were still far out on the water. The other girls came to her to ask what to do.

A man alone, walking on the beach, a stranger; White Hare wondered how this could be. He looked startled when he saw the maidens.

His shiny black hair was brought up in a holder of some kind which made his head seem oddly shaped. His garment was definitely not made of animal skin or any plant she had ever seen. White Hare could not guess what it might be, but it was more gaily colored than the plumage of birds. He had necklaces hanging down his chest, and large round earrings, a combination of seashell stones, shiny yellow amulets and feathers. She had never seen anyone like him.

It was not more than a moment after his initial surprise that he regained his composure. He stood still and beckoned for them to come closer to him. He smiled to the girls, holding his hands far from his spear holder.

White Hare stood. "He must be lost," she told the others. "I wonder where he's from and what he's doing here. Let's go find out."

The girls approached timidly. The man allowed them to touch the strange fabric of his garment. The young ones laughed at the feel of the smooth, dyed cotton. The gold at the man's neck and ears glittered. He seemed rather like a large bird. White Hare motioned the children back. This was not a dignified way to greet a stranger. She wondered how her mother or one of the elders would manage, but it was up to her to say the first words.

"Welcome to the land of the Chumash," she said formally. "I am White Hare, the eldest of my companions. Who are you?"

She waited, but there was no reply at first. Then he opened his mouth to speak, but his words were ones they had never heard before. After he finished his small speech, the girls looked at each other and back to him, wondering what to do. It was clear there was going to be a problem with communication. White Hare pointed to herself and said, "White Hare." Then she pointed to him and waited.

"Toacoatl," he replied.

"He must be lost. He doesn't look or sound anything like our people."

"Could he be from one of the Shoshoni tribes?" one of the girls questioned. "They come from over the desert, from the highest mountain ranges and the plains. Some of their families live in our mountains. He might be a relative coming to visit."

"I don't think so," another answered. "That doesn't sound like their speech. My cousin is married to one."

"He's not a Tongva from the Big Valley either," White Hare added." They don't look so outlandish."

By now, the man was looking from one to the other of them. Someone had to do something, White Hare decided. "I guess we ought to do something friendly," she said. "Let's offer him some food. That's always a good idea. He might be hungry. Little Goat, go get some clams from one of the baskets, and bring fresh water." The little girl hurried to obey.

Toacoatl took the clam that White Hare opened for him with her small serrated shell knife. He made a little bow, signifying that he understood it for the offer of friendship. He ate and drank, but except when his head was back to drink from the skin, he kept his eyes on White Hare. He stared at her quite oddly for a long moment before his gaze shifted. Then he pointed south and said something in his own tongue. The girls shook their heads. There was something he needed to say, but he was at a loss as to how to say it. It sounded like a request. Whether it was for information or an item, they could not guess.

At last, he bent down and smoothed out some sand. With all the girls standing around him and watching, he drew stick figures and he pointed down the beach past the turn of the inlet. He looked back at them expectantly.

"He has friends waiting down the beach," Climber called out. "He must want us to meet them."

"Do you think we ought to?" one of the other girls asked.

The boys out on the water must have noticed the strangers. They were swiftly approaching in the tomols. Dancing Bear was the first to debark. The boys pulled the boats up and under the small cliffs and tied them to posts so they would be safe from the tides. The nets were quickly emptied into the waiting baskets. White Hare waited for them all to arrive. It was easier to act brave when there were twenty maidens and one man. The prospect of more strangers daunted her. But having Dancing Bear close made her feel safe. She chided herself for her timidity.

"This stranger does not speak Hokan or Tak'lit, the

language of the Shoshoni," she told the boys. "He has shown us by means of this picture on the sand that he has companions on the other side of the beach."

"We saw them from the boats. That's why we came in."

"What do you think we should do?"

"I guess we ought to go look at them. There are enough of us. My father went on a trading expedition a long time ago and told me about some of the eastern peoples. I wonder if they're Hopi traders. It would be strange that they'd come all the way to the ocean to trade unless they're looking for Muwu Town up the coast."

Dancing Bear and White Hare led the group. It felt peculiar to White Hare to be able to talk and not be understood. Toacoatl stood right beside them and yet she could speak privately. She felt safe in asking Dancing Bear before they reached the outcropping of rocks, "Do you think there may be any danger? We're responsible for the children."

"I have my shell carving knife. A few other boys have bone knives and fishing spears. The strangers are most probably traders. Who else would be wandering far from home?" White Hare did not answer, so he went on. "In any case, we'll be careful."

White Hare smiled weakly as they rounded the bend. There were about a dozen men milling about a large tent set against the small cliff. She saw three women near a fire roasting what looked like antelope. The men were engaged in various chores, sharpening knives of horn or bone, and affixing obsidian darts to arrows. They appeared surprised to see the newcomers. They hurried to stand together with their weapons as Toacoatl left White Hare and the others to go and speak to them.

Each group observed the other with caution and curiosity. Toacoatl's people were covered breast to knee in clothes of many colors. Their hair and decorations were as ornate as if they were celebrating a holiday. Some of the men had markings on their cheeks and chins in blues and reds. It seemed quite deforming. White Hare realized their foreheads were oddly shaped. It was not only the effect of how they wore their hair. Their noses were odd too.

She moved closer to Dancing Bear. "Do you understand any of their words?" she asked. "Does it sound like the Hopi language?"

"No. Besides, traders usually don't go as far as Muwu Town. It's just too far for the easterners. They can't be from the north. It's all Chumash land for a month's journey. They must be from the far south."

There was no common language, then, that they could use to speak to each other. There was only so much that could be said in sand drawings, although White Hare thought it was clever of Toacoatl to think of it. He drew skillfully and fast.

Sand, one of the boys who was standing near Dancing Bear, spoke. "Since they've come from a far place, it would be polite for us to invite them to spend the night at our village. Maybe they do have some things for trading."

"Why don't you run up to the village and tell them we might be bringing home some extras for supper," Dancing Bear suggested to him. "We can manage the baskets so you can travel light."

"I'll do that." The boy grinned and began up the steep path.

"I'm not too sure I want them to visit. I don't like the way their men look at me." White Hare gave an involuntary shudder. The men were now staring blatantly and impolitely both at her and at the other maidens. "Their women are all covered up. They seem to be shocked that we're bare. Do they expect us to wear capes in hot weather? You'd think they'd never seen women before. I never feel so strange when you look at me."

Dancing Bear had no chance to answer. Just then a boy of about fifteen summers came walking down to the beach from the grassy slope above them. The Chumash were shocked to see that he was leading four large animals by rawhide straps that were tied around their faces and necks.

Climber gave a shriek and her twin, Little Goat, scampered high up onto the rocks. The twins were so much alike in their reaction, White Hare almost wanted to laugh, but her own fear of the great beasts restrained her. "What are they?" she asked.

Dancing Bear stepped back himself. "They must be some kind of deer, but I never saw deer or antelope with faces like that, so long and broad. They have no antlers. There's hair like human hair on their necks and a tail like no antelope's I ever saw."

"I never heard of antelope you could lead on ropes, either," Yellow Flower, one of the maidens, added.

The animals greeted the foreigners with snorts and whinnies, breaking up the discussion as they were patted and tethered to the lodgepoles of the tent. The largest of the beasts was male, White Hare noticed, and black as obsidian. He stood the tallest and looked around with huge, round eyes over the backs of the lighter-colored females.

Toacoatl approached the Chumash young people again, smiling. He pointed to the four beasts and said, "Horses." They repeated the word. Then he pointed to the fire and the women carving up the meat. They offered to share their meal and their water.

White Hare's original estimate of a lost, hungry wanderer was far off the mark, she realized, as one of the women handed her a shell with sizzling hunks of meat. The sight and smell of all that meat made her mouth water. Soon, all of them were sitting and enjoying the feast with their unusual hosts.

"I wonder if they herd those horses the way some of the nations keep rabbits or goats or dogs for food, and if this meat we're eating is horse," Dancing Bear said. He raised the joint of meat he was working on and called out, "Toacoatl!" He motioned toward the great beasts. "Horses?"

Toacoatl laughed until he began to cough on a piece of meat. The other strangers laughed also, shaking their heads. A few of the men made faces as if they tasted something bad.

"I guess this really is antelope," Dancing Bear stated. He was slightly put off by the laughter. "But, how was I to know?"

After they ate and washed the grease off their hands and faces in the ocean, Toacoatl rose and came over to Dancing Bear. He seemed to take him for their leader now. Perhaps he was trying to appease him for the humiliation of being laughed at. White Hare, being of the same age as Dancing Bear and equal in status, was not pleased.

With no language in common, Toacoatl's communication consisted of a conglomeration of gestures. He pointed first at his people and the horses, then at the band of young Chumash. He motioned for the Chumash to begin to walk and pointed to his own people again. Then, he gave a few terse commands to his group. The women began to pack everything up and take down the tent while the men lined up the horses and saw to the carrying of their weapons.

"They are coming with us," Dancing Bear said, "whether we invite them or not. I guess that's what comes of not being able to understand each other. Well, if they conduct themselves peaceably, it will be nice to have visitors. We have plenty of fish and shellfood. Some of the women went to gather chia and bulbs yesterday, so we'll have something besides acorn mush to eat with the stew. It would be nice to have a feast and stories around the fire. It's two more months until summer solstice. We could do with a holiday."

The women were by now quite busy loading the beasts as if there were no doubt of the Chumash decision. The horses stood patiently, their wide eyes alert. They made soft, snorting noises and shook their heads, but they did not seem to object when bundles were laid on them and drag poles attached to carry the heavy skins that were the tent coverings. The tallest men held the lead ropes to guide them.

"They look like huge grazers," Yellow Flower said, "but they're not frightened of people. I imagine they can fight well with hooves like that, but they carry burdens and let men lead them on ropes. How strange!"

They were only a short way up the steep path when the first of the problems occurred. The path became too steep and narrow for the travois tied behind the stallion. It leaned over the edge even as Toacoatl guided the horse's hooves. A few of the bundles fell off and over the steep incline until they were stopped by the rocks and bushes below.

The Chumash had their hands free since the baskets were carried on their backs and shoulders, but they were weighted down. Pebbles and clumps of grass fell as the horses struggled, and the path was even narrower farther ahead. Toacoatl motioned for the Chumash youngsters in the lead and called out in his own language until one of the men went back for the bundles.

"This isn't going to work," White Hare called out to Dancing Bear. She walked with the girls and the women. "They can never make it up this path. We have to take them back down and go by an easier route."

With Dancing Bear and the other boys to help, the horses were turned, not without difficulty. A few of the drag poles fell, and bundles had to be retrieved again.

Wolf, one of the oldest boys, said, "I don't think these animals can climb the narrow, rocky path to Simo'mo even if we can get them to the meadow below it. Let's help them to the grassland there and only bring a few of the strangers to meet with our wot and the antap council. The rest can stay below to protect their animals until we know what to do about them."

"And protect us *from* their animals," Little Goat said, laughing. A few of the Chumash reached out to try to touch the horses, but withdrew when the mares showed their teeth.

After they had been walking a while, White Hare looked closely at the three women who walked behind the men and the horses in the line. They carried most of the bundles which were not already on the horses. They were covered neck to knees with a woven, sand-colored material, quite drab and undecorated. They all had fatigue lines and sweat running down their faces. One looked to be not much older than Pink Shell. Where the other two sank beneath their burdens so as to be noticed little, this one looked about her inquisitively, stately, even as she struggled with her packs.

White Hare walked over to her and touched her dress, smiling shyly to reassure her that she meant no harm. The woman backed into her companions at first, frightened. Then she stood still under White Hare's inspection.

"I won't hurt you," White Hare said, knowing she would not be understood, but wanting to be accepted. "What is this stuff?" She indicated the fabric.

The woman returned her smile and seemed to understand. "Cotton," she answered. The Chumash girls repeated the word. It might not be that hard to learn to understand each other.

The other women grew bolder at this exchange and fingered White Hare and Yellow Flower's short skirts. Then, they tried to repeat White Hare's question, not quite getting the words right. It sounded like "Whas-tuff?" The little girls laughed.

"Yucca fibers." She didn't want to say too much at one time and confuse them. Naming things was the right way to start.

The youngest woman's name was Mara. The other two were called Rasha and Sena. With bundles on head and back, managing the trail was difficult even for one who was used to the mountains. Although Mara managed skillfully, there was a tiredness in her eyes. The journey seemed to hold no pleasure for her and the other women who trudged along. A few days' rest would fix them up, White Hare guessed.

The roundabout way up to the village was taking longer, but gave the horses no trouble. They were strong beasts. The group would still arrive before sundown. The men's and boys' spirited voices indicated that they, too, were trying to communicate. White Hare hoped the elders would not object to the visit.

There was so much that she wanted to ask the women, it annoyed her that they could not understand her. With her free hand, she began to point things out to them.

"Hawk," she said pointing up as one floated by on a current of air.

"Hawk," Mara repeated with a smile, understanding that White Hare wanted her to learn the word.

"Flower," White Hare said as they passed a clump of bright blue lupines that bordered the path.

Mara followed her pointing finger with her eyes and repeated her words. Whether it was that the others were not so keen to learn or only more exhausted, it was Mara who tried to learn.

The group walked past a small village much closer to the shore than their own. White Hare pointed out a keesh and said the word for it. The older women seemed to light up at last as they stopped.

"Not here," White Hare told them. "We go much farther, but we can sit and rest awhile." She wished she had a way to tell them that this was not home. She shook her head, but she was not sure they understood even that simple gesture. She might be confusing them. Down the trail, it seemed the boys were having a similar problem.

Villagers came pouring out of their huts and began to holler to each other as soon as they saw the horses. Men ran back for bows and arrows and women screamed as the horses reared, frightened of the noise. It took the combined explanations of the Chumash young people from Simo'mo and the skill of the foreigners to calm the villagers and the animals. White Hare hoped her family and friends were not going to panic the way these villagers did. They had been told to expect guests, but Sand, whom Dancing Bear had sent ahead, had not seen the strange beasts that the foreigners commanded.

The group reached a wide, grassy plain below the hills of the village where Dancing Bear indicated that the horses might remain. The men unloaded the burdens from the animals. Before they began to set up their tent, White Hare saw that the front legs of the horses were being tied together with ropes from one of the sacks so that they would not run. She shook her head in amazement that such beasts could be so controlled. She would as much try to control a mountain lion.

Council

The villagers of Simo'mo stood above them on the hills as they arrived with the strangers. Black Raven, the alchuklash, was the first to touch the hands of the visitors in greeting. Gray Eagle, the wot, was just behind him. He muttered welcomes and demonstrated as he spoke where they were to leave their bundles so he could bring them to the large sweathouse, the temescal, where they could be made clean and purified from their journey.

"They don't understand you," Dancing Bear told him. "Their language is different from any I ever heard. You have to use motions."

Gray Eagle considered for a moment. "They will understand clean if they are civilized and rest if they are tired and food if they are hungry." He motioned to the men to follow him.

Toacoatl nodded, understanding enough apparently to give orders to one of his people to guard their few belongings. The rest were below where the women and those men left behind were erecting the large tent.

Everyone had questions. Yellow Flower ran to her mother to explain. The twins were talking at once. Women were hurrying to prepare food and rushing around. White Hare stood still as Blue Star listened quietly to everyone else. She was a wise woman now, having been initiated into some of the minor mysteries. "I think," Blue Star said, "that the women will be in need of cleansing also. Will some of you walk down with me to bring them to the women's temescal?"

She led the girls down the hill. The three women were laying the skins over the lodgepoles. White Hare had never seen so large a tent. It was longer than it was high, and it was divided into three sections. The girls hurried to help the women and soon the structure was standing as it stood on the beach. The women looked ready to drop from the their long climb and the work of tent making, but still they did most of the work while the men who stayed behind to guard the horses only watched.

Before the women could begin the placement of whatever belongings were in the bundles, Blue Star made them stop. "Remember," White Hare said, "They can't understand us."

Blue Star put both hands on one of the women's shoulders and held her still. Then she made a sharp cutting-off motion with one hand and pointed to the bundles as if to tell the women to leave them where they were. "Come with me," she said, using her hands now in a sweeping motion as if she were gathering the women behind her. "Bring them," she added. She was not taking any chances. "They smell. I won't have them bringing lice into the village. Besides, a steam bath will do them good. They've been traveling a long time."

The girls took the women's hands and brought them up the hill. In the courtyard of the temescal, Blue Star took off her skirt and told the girls to do likewise. Then she motioned for the foreign women to remove their tunics. The three undressed shyly. A few of the village women helped them, holding their noses. The grime and fleas of long journeying were rubbed off with lathered yucca root and gourds of water lifted from a large watertight basket were poured over them.

The women seemed amazed to be waited on. Old dry robes were wrapped around them to keep them from becoming chilled until they could enter the temescal. Mara knelt and took Blue Star's hand, pressing it to her cheek.

The other women did the same. Yellow Flower nudged White Hare and whispered. "Isn't that a little too much to say thank you for normal hospitality?"

"We don't know their customs. Shh," White Hare answered.

When they were inside, Blue Star lit a clump of dried white sage, the plant of ritual purification. She put the leaves into a large abalone bowl and said a prayer to Mother Earth in the sacred language. She held the bowl under the women's noses so they could inhale the sharp fragrance. She passed the bowl slowly around their bodies, then toward the four sacred directions, and handed it to White Hare. She passed the smoke-filled shell around her body too before handing it to the next girl.

It was dim in this special keesh. The temescal was lower than the homes. A pit was dug in the center where hot coals were kept burning. When the ritual purification was complete, Blue Star had the foreign women sit by the pit with their legs over the edge.

"White Hare, get water from the basket and pour it slowly over the coals," she directed.

White Hare took the gourd of water and returned. As she poured, the coals sizzled loudly and hot clouds of steam filled the room. Everyone breathed deeply. The only sounds were the sighs of the foreign women and the sizzle of the hot rocks on the coals.

White Hare's skin began to tingle from the heat. The steam felt so good after her long hike from the sea. She could almost imagine the fatigue the women were feeling and how the steam was soothing them, entering into their skin and giving them relief.

"Into the stream now, everyone," Blue Star commanded.

By now, the girls knew the names of the foreigners. White Hare was the first into the water, followed by Yellow Flower. Goat and Climber and the others were soon splashing and laughing as they cooled down. Mother guided the women to the edge of the water. Sena gasped as she stepped into the stream. Hands reached out to help pull her in. Rasha walked in stoically. The water was not really cold; it only felt so at first after the heat. She got down quickly even though she shivered. Then she sighed deeply and some of her fatigue lines softened.

"Come on," Yellow Flower urged Mara, who stood hesitating at the edge of the stream. "It feels better if you get in all at once."

"You know she doesn't understand you," White Hare reminded her. She got out of the water and walked up

"People are looking out of holes in the walls!" White Hare said as quietly as she could manage to the girls around her. "What a strange idea!"

Toacoatl made the first drawing carefully. Then he did simple representations of others. Half of Simo'mo could fit into one of these huge houses, if houses they were. Away from these, Toacoatl drew what looked like a strange mountain with zigzagging walkways going up to a square house on the summit.

Black Raven took the stick and drew sky figures and lightning. Toacoatl smiled at last and said something in his odd language.

"God houses," Black Raven said triumphantly to his audience. "They are made by people and they are stone."

"Stone!" "People make mountains!" Mutters were heard all around them.

"Quiet," Black Raven demanded, holding up a hand. The murmurs died away. To Toacoatl, the alchuklash said one word. "Aztec?"

The foreign leader grinned. To White Hare, the man's teeth only made his nose look sharper and more hooked, like the beak of an eagle. She wondered how she could have thought him handsome at first.

"No one has come to us from one of the great cities since my father was a boy," Black Raven explained to Gray Eagle and the antap council. "I was with my father in Muwu when a group of Aztec merchants and traders came through on their way home. They traded for some of our beautiful waterproof baskets and obsidian from the islands. You all know Muwu." He looked around at his audience. "If you took Muwu and

Sumo and Wenemmu and piled Syuxtun, the northern capital, on top of them, you would have a city that could be equal in size to the cities these people control."

"But what are they doing here?" Gray Eagle insisted. "They don't seem like traders. This is a long way from home for them. What is their destination? See if you can find out more."

Toacoatl rubbed out his picture of the city. Again, White Hare felt the hairs stand up on her neck. If drawing a cloud could help to bring the rain and drawing antelope could bring luck on a hunt, could the rubbing out of pictures of her home village and the southern city mean a disaster would someday destroy these two places? Drawing seemed too much like magic. White Hare reprimanded herself for having such a terrible thought. Wise priests knew better than an untrained maiden of fifteen summers.

Toacoatl was using the stick again. As he stood away, White Hare saw a representation of a powerful-looking man with many feathers in his headdress. From the first man, he drew a line to a smaller one. The second man also wore regal feathers. When he had everyone's attention, he stood tall and smiling. He pointed with great emphasis to the smaller figure and then to himself. He said something in his own tongue and stood somewhat arrogantly, knuckles on his hips.

Black Raven said, "He says he's a great man, son of a greater man, perhaps a ruler in such a city as he has shown us."

Toacoatl said more. Then his own people knelt before him and touched the ground with their foreheads. There were gasps from the Chumash. Never was the highest-ranking alchuklash or wot so high above his people that they needed to abase themselves in such a manner before him.

Gray Eagle said to Black Raven, "Why does a man as high and mighty as this come so far from home? To see the sights with his followers? I don't think so. There is more to discover."

"The stories say the Aztec are a warlike people," Black Raven told him. "They have conquered many nations in the south and made an empire of them. They all owe allegiance to one wot, whom they call an emperor. This man could be a king or a prince of one of the smaller countries or his emissary come to negotiate with us."

"No," Gray Eagle replied. "He found us by accident. He would have brought presents if that was his mission. He may be a spy, here to guess our strength, to report to his emperor if we are worth conquering. It may be best not to anger them, but I don't trust people I can't understand. What do you suggest?"

Black Raven rubbed his thin grey mustache while he thought. White Hare realized none of the men in the party of foreigners had facial hair. Come to think of it, visitors from other nations seldom did.

"They are too small to be a war party," Black Raven said after a while. "There is more to learn, as you say. I will drink the sacred datura and see what dreams it gives me, but it will be difficult to penetrate their motives. We don't know their language. Perhaps the foreigners will want to continue their journey after they rest for a few days, and our concern will have been for nothing. Let them stay for now while we think and study them."

Gray Eagle nodded.

While her wot and alchuklash conferred softly, White Hare watched the strangers. She and the women were in the shadows, barely seen by the participants in the council, but she saw things the men might have missed. She noticed the resigned look on most of the foreign men's faces as they made their bows. She also noticed that the women, who were pulled forward when Toacoatl gave his commands, held their drying robes tightly around them. All three of them held their faces almost as stiffly as they held the robes, but Mara's teeth were clenched. Toacoatl, who looked above their heads, never saw.

Gray Eagle rose to his feet and gestured toward the outside to their visitors. "Come and have supper with my people," he said in a gracious voice. They understood enough to follow him. They were going to be allowed to visit and their encampment was not going to be challenged.

The antap brought them to a place of honor near the fire. Black Raven told the group who found them to make them comfortable and bring them food. The younger boys and girls ran for mats.

White Hare and the others took wooden bowls to the cooking baskets. The women added white hot stones from the fire to the fish stew to keep it boiling. Fish and clams and mussels were thickened with chia in a broth flavored with sage and wild onions and mushrooms. It was a dish they could serve to guests with pride. Acorn mush was ladled onto hot rocks by the fire to harden into flat, crunchy bread for dipping in the stew.

On hearing that there were to be guests, some of the

young children ran to gather some of the prickly pear fruit. Since there had been no time to soak it to bring out the thorns, people held the fruit on pointed sticks.

"This isn't bad," Dancing Bear remarked to White Hare as they began on their own food. "Two feasts in one day."

"If we keep up this kind of eating, we'll get fat," White Hare answered with a laugh.

It was a good dinner, but she wondered how meager it must seem to one who came from a huge city and who might be as important there as this Toacoatl claimed to be. She was glad to see the women eating well. They were thin enough. On this journey of theirs, at least, a surplus of food was not an everyday happening.

White Hare wondered about many things as she helped to serve the guests. She wondered if there was more Toacoatl would have tried to communicate if Gray Eagle had not ended the council meeting when he did. She wondered what the foreigners thought of her little village and its people. She also wondered why Mara clenched her teeth.

Learning

When White Hare was not out gathering seeds and digging roots during the first days of the visitors' stay, she spent all the time she could observing them. They were different from Chumash men in many ways, not only in the way they looked. For instance, they were more organized.

One of the first things the Aztec men did was to hack down many small trees with their axes to fashion an enclosure for their horses. The horses used up much of their time. Even after the enclosure was complete with its small gate, the foreigners spent an excessive amount of energy grooming and feeding and decorating them. They were beasts of burden and useful. Evidently, the Aztecs valued them.

It soon was obvious that the mares were pregnant. The Aztec guards kept the villagers away from them. A band of children tried to sneak down one night, soon after the strangers arrived, but they were sent scurrying back to their beds by the Aztecs, from the tent who came rushing out with spears when the guards called.

Except for the strange behavior concerning their animals, the foreign men were polite as it was possible to be with no language in common. They seldom visited the village after the first night, but remained in or near their tent. They made no move to continue their journey.

At first, White Hare assumed the women to be wives to the men. What else could they be? The two oldest, Sena and Rasha, went to gather acorns and roots with the village women. They watched how the village women prepared the acorns, pounding them into meal and laying the meal over leaves in loosely woven, untreated baskets so the water they poured over the meal could wash out the bitterness. It wasn't hard, but it required patience.

Mara, the youngest, saw White Hare and others preparing to go down to the beach and ran to ask with her few Chumash words and signs if she might go with them. White Hare smiled to her and said, "Wait," before she ran back to her keesh to bring out an extra basket. She helped the foreign woman adjust it, with the band on her forehead, so it could rest comfortably on her back.

The steep, winding path that led down to the beach was bordered by the short, squat plants with spidery leaves and the giant yellow blooms that White Hare loved to see. The thick stems and leaves were the color of deep spring. The flowers would dry up and be gone before true summer was really upon them. The sky was turquoise blue and the ocean, when she could see it from the meadow before the path took them out of sight of it, looked green and calm.

The path took them past the great shell rock. It was one with deep impressions of oyster and clam shells in hard rock. The Chumash band saw it often. Mara stopped, amazed.

White Hare saw her stare at the rock with disbelief. "It's all right," she said, trying to soothe her. "I know it looks impossible, but it's not bad magic." White Hare motioned for her to go on, not to hold up the line on the narrow path.

"I wish I could explain it to her," White Hare said to Yellow Flower as they continued.

"Do you think she would understand about the Swordfish People who live under the sea? Do you think you could make her understand about Old Man Coyote getting them mad with his tricks until they threw a clump of mud at him when he escaped from their trap and laughed at them from up here on this path? Do you think she would believe that the shell creatures fell off, but their shapes remained when the mud turned to rock? She'll be gone long before she learns enough words."

"I wish she could at least tell us where they were going before we found them, though. She's catching on to a lot of our words, but she doesn't seem to understand me when I ask her that."

White Hare was not only teaching Mara. She herself was learning a little of the language the young woman spoke. Once she told Mara the Chumash word for a thing, she would not leave it until she learned Mara's word. By now, she could say, "It's a hot day," and "There's a big clam," without thinking. She caught on faster than her friends. It was pleasing to discover that she had the knack for learning, and it was fun to use the different words. White Hare wondered if Mara was teaching Hokan, the Chumash language, to her men.

Gray Eagle and the council gave the word to the villagers that they were to continue to be courteous to the foreigners when they met. If, using his powers, Black Raven was able to discover more about them, it had not been made known to the rest of them.

One evening, a few of White Hare's friends were gathered in front of Pink Shell's keesh. Red Antler was playing guess-which-hand-hid-the-stick. Yellow Flower had a pile of beads and flowers already won from Dancing Bear resting by her side. Pink Shell was nursing Wiggler.

Red Antler passed the stick between his hands, making passes and turns to confuse them. Then he held both hands closed before him. Yellow Flower guessed first since she was the previous winner, leaving White Hare to guess the other hand. Red Antler opened two hands to show them Yellow Flower had guessed right again.

"You're not concentrating," Dancing Bear said. "Sit back. I'm not going to let Yellow Flower win everything in sight. For a small basket of blackberries, Yellow Flower?"

She nodded.

"Place your bets," Red Antler said with a grin. He waited until they were ready. "Now." His hands closed. Faster and faster they moved, making a blur until White Hare had no idea where the stick was. She bet with Yellow Flower. If the girl lost, White Hare would have to help decorate Dancing Bear's home with flowers for Solstice Day. It was a task she enjoyed, but it helped to spice the bets when there was something at stake.

Red Antler held out his closed hands to Dancing Bear, since it was his challenge. If Yellow Flower chose the same hand, the game had to be repeated. She chose the other. Red Antler's hands opened, revealing the stick in the one Dancing Bear picked.

"You can gather my blackberries tomorrow, Yellow Flower," Dancing Bear said, yawning as if beating her at guessing was an every day occurrence. "And White Hare, just make sure you have the flowers there in plenty of time, something bright and cheerful. A few hollyleaf redberries would look nice along with some larkspurs. See if you can find some fir branches, too. My mother likes those."

"You were lucky. Wait until next time," Yellow Flower said, laughing. "Oh, look!" She pointed down the hill.

One of the mares within the enclosure was lying on its side and making shrill sounds as its sides heaved with the contractions of birth. Pink Shell picked up Wiggler, who was reaching for one of Yellow Flower's strands of beads, and slung him over one hip. "White Hare?" She looked at her friend.

White Hare grabbed Wiggler's brother, Frog, and propped him on her hip as they all ran down the hill. The foreigners could not very well chase the whole village away. Most of them were there already, near the corral, the children pushing their faces against the fence.

The foreign men, at least a majority of them, stood inside the enclosure, watching and looking frightened as the mare heaved and cried. The other two mares stood away from the people. The stallion paced and pawed the ground.

The mare continued to cry with her contractions. An old, white-haired woman came up close to the gate and yelled out to the men. They heard her, but they looked as if they did not know whether to chase her away or let her come closer. It was the old antap woman who had been with Grandfather when he died. White Hare knew the woman had great powers of healing. True, she could not help Grandfather and a horse was something she had never seen, but if anyone could help it was she, yet she was unable to make the Aztecs understand her.

White Hare rushed to where she saw Mara waiting. "Tell them she wants to help," she shouted. "Make them understand that she can help!"

The young woman ran to where the men could see her and shouted in their own language. Toacoatl shrugged and then shouted something back. He motioned with his hand and his men opened the gate long enough for the woman to enter.

The antap woman was stronger than she looked. As the foreigners and the village watched, she reached into the struggling mare and guided the foal with her hands. A short time later, the foal, enclosed in its wet and shiny placental sac, emerged from its mother.

The priestess broke the sac and pulled it away from the wet, lanky creature. She wiped the fluid from its nostrils with a goatskin rag from her belt. The stallion came over to inspect and smell the foal and the woman moved away, toward the gate. "It's a male," she told the assembled villagers. The foreigners could see for themselves.

The stallion began to lick the newborn dry with his tongue. Soon the mare stood and the two of them continued to clean and dry him. No one wanted to leave. This time, at least, the foreigners could do nothing about it, not after they had accepted the old woman's help.

After only a short time and one mishap when the foal sprawled back onto the ground, the tiny foal was standing alongside his mother and looking for his first meal.

"It's amazing. It's wonderful." Pink Shell and Yellow Flower were talking at the same time. By now the sun was far below the horizon and only a little pink showed at its westernmost base in the blue-black sky. The stars shone like flakes of crystal, and a crescent moon was rising. They walked back to the village.

"I'm glad the old birth woman was there to help. The female and her baby might have died without her." White Hare still felt the magic.

"They should be glad you were there to help," Pink Shell said proudly, putting one arm around White Hare's shoulders. She held Wiggler, fast asleep on her breast. Red Antler held his other son.

"Me?" White Hare asked. "What did I do?"

"You made them understand that she *could* help. You spoke in Mara's language."

In her excitement, White Hare had not realized the words she spoke were not her own. A warm blush came to her cheeks.

It was a thing that was hard to understand and White Hare thought about it that night before she fell asleep. Sometimes, when she was excited, she did something she could not explain later. It might be pushing down

the leader of a gang of boys or it might be calling forth
words to speak that she barely knew. Yet, without anger or fear or excitement to drive her, she was timid,
afraid to confront anyone, shy.

It was another thing to realize that she never heard
of anyone talking to the dying without words since her
own experience. She wondered sometimes, if she only
dreamed the things Grandfather told her in the cave
before he died. It seemed like a dream now; it was so
long ago. The priestess was not surprised. She told her
he wanted to "talk" to her when he could not talk. But
the antap priests and priestesses often took the datura
potion. It gave them their dreams and power and
knowledge. They could see and hear things that the
ordinary people could not, but then, what could account for her ability? Grandfather said he wanted to
speak to Mother also. Was it a special gift then, one
that was passed down within her family? Mother never
spoke of it.

Now that day had turned to only fragments in her
memory, brought to mind by, certain words and
phrases. *Strangers* was one of the words in Grandfather's warning. She wondered if her grandfather had had
the gift of prophecy. If he did, he had still never asked
to be admitted into the antap. She was sure they would
not have refused. It was something, therefore, that she
would never do either. Grandfather was content to be
one of the ordinary folk of the People. If being ordinary
was good enough for him, it was good enough for her.

One evening, Blue Star invited the foreign women
to come to their keesh after the evening meal. There
was still plenty of light during the longer days of approaching summer and the cool of the evening before

it grew dark. It was the best time to work. Blue Star needed to make her new baskets waterproof.

By now, Sena and Rasha and Mara had seen the way the Chumash women cooked. White Hare made tea for them while Blue Star waited for the asphaltum to melt in the large stone by the fire. It was a stone White Hare's father, Goat Killer, had found for Blue Star once, and she kept it in a corner of the keesh, under a bed.

White Hare pulled heated stones from the fire with two sticks and plopped them with a hiss into the small water-filled basket. These were only small stones, but just a few of them could make the water boil. White Hare sprinkled mint and sour berry into the water and stirred. Then she let the tea steep while she went into the keesh for the precious pottery.

"What is the point of having something you never use at all?" was her argument to Blue Star and her mother agreed. The foreign women held the cups and inhaled the delicious smell. Every kindness seemed to have a major effect on them. It was one of the reasons White Hare felt drawn to them, she imagined.

The tarry asphaltum began to bubble.

"Now, watch," Blue Star said. She threw scores of tiny pebbles into the hot, sticky tar. Then she lowered in a shell tied to a handle with yucca cord to the mess and withdrew the pebbles, throwing them immediately into the one of the baskets. She shook the basket vigorously for a short time, then poured the pebbles back into the tar. The basket was done.

Sena and Rasha and Mara each lifted the basket and peered within. There was a fine coating of asphaltum already cooling and hardening and making the basket twice as useful.

"Good," Rasha said. She, too, was attempting to speak the language of her hosts.

"Very good," Sena echoed.

"And easy," Mara added.

White Hare felt proud of her people, especially now. This was a thing people from a large, stone city had traveled far to see and trade for in the days of Black Raven's childhood. Her people were also superior in knowing the ways of peace from what the alchuklash told them.

Not only were the southern women amazed at their crafts, they also began to dress like the Chumash women. Their cotton tunics were in rags when they arrived, and washing made them fall completely apart. Even the sinew they used could not darn them and it was only practical to use what was available. After a while, their men forgot to stare. It must be as Dancing Bear suggested. They were merely unused to the scantier, freer Chumash manner of dress.

It was a week later when the three women were able to leave their tasks and come to visit again. White Hare and Yellow Flower were in front of Pink Shell's keesh with her when the women walked up hesitantly.

"Come over," Pink Shell called to them, beckoning with her hand. "Look how Frog and Wiggler are growing." Yellow Flower and White Hare had to work to keep the babies from crawling away while they brushed the babies' hair with shell combs. The boys could already pull themselves up to stand, and they were anxious to explore. It took everyone's attention to keep them out of trouble.

Pink Shell's keesh was decorated with flowers and

leaves and woven hangings. "Holiday time is coming," White Hare said.

"We'll eat so much, we'll all get fat," Yellow Flower said, demonstrating her tummy growing bigger to make sure they understood her. She laughed and Mara laughed too. The other women smiled and nodded, but White Hare suspected they had less understanding of what Yellow Flower was trying to say. The gesture might be the same if she was trying to tell them that she was pregnant.

She was glad, though, that Mara caught on. It was good to see her happy for a change. So often, she looked sad. It was just a little thing, something about the expression in her eyes even when she smiled. White Hare wondered if Mara was homesick.

"There will be games," she added to what Yellow Flower had to say. She pointed to a gaming stick laying nearby. Everyone loved gambling. By now Mara and Sena and Rasha had seen them play often enough to understand. "And dances." She did a few whirls.

Yellow Flower added, "It's a time for pairing and courting also. I wonder whether Dancing Bear picked someone yet."

"Are you going to ask him?" White Hare asked too quickly.

Yellow Flower smiled. "No. I was only wondering. I won't ask him if you want to, but you'd better make up your mind soon or somebody else might. I think Otter Girl has her eye on him."

"Otter Girl!" White Hare put her hand up to her mouth wishing she had enough sense to say nothing instead of reacting so fast no one had to guess what she was thinking.

Pink Shell came out of her keesh, carrying Frog. She had been listening inside. "Be careful, White Hare," she warned, sitting down with her baby on her lap. "If you become too friendly with Dancing Bear, you'll be taking care of your own little one soon and pounding acorns with the rest of us old women." The friends laughed and hugged each other as Wiggler crawled out and plopped himself down on White Hare. She tickled him and laughed herself because his laugh was so catching.

"Maybe it would not be so bad," White Hare said thoughtfully. "You're happy, aren't you?"

Pink Shell smiled a very grown-up smile. "Being a wife and a mother isn't the end of the world, you know. Sometimes, my mother watches the boys so Red Antler and I can go down to the beach for a few days to camp out and be alone. I can still enjoy my beautiful beach and a few other things as well."

"Before you know it, there'll be more babies to take care of." Yellow Flower made a funny face.

"You're a baby. You don't know everything," Pink Shell countered.

"Do you have holidays?" White Hare asked their guests. She was beginning to be annoyed at the way the conversation was going. Besides, it was impolite to their guests to say so much they could not understand.

"Holidays." Mara said the word very slowly as if tasting it. Surely, she had caught the meaning of the word by now. "In my home are bad holidays. Bad gods; many killings." White Hare and the other Chumash women could not know then that she used the word used by hunters as in "I killed a goat." She did not know the word for sacrifices.

"You hunt for your gods?" Yellow Flower asked, surprised. "We give ours seeds and flowers."

"Hunt people and babies," she said, pointing to Wiggler and Frog.

"No!" White Hare exclaimed. "You don't know the right words. You can't mean that."

Mara did not try to speak again. She seemed to withdraw.

Breaking the silence, Yellow Flower brightened and pointed down the hill. Toacoatl was mounted on the stallion; the youngest man, whom they now knew to be his brother, was on one of the mares. All the foals were born now. A group of the Aztec men came together to leave half a deer before the siliak in the center of the village. When the antap priests and priestesses came running out to see why the dogs were barking, Toacoatl said in heavily accented Hokan, "For the woman."

After this, the antap felt more kindly toward the foreigners in general. Goat Killer did not. "I wish they would take their strange beasts and go away," he said one day shortly after the foals' births.

White Hare did not like to give up her friends, but she could not exactly blame her father. From pieces of conversations she heard, many of the other villagers felt the same. There was something . . . not right about the feeling she got from the Aztec men. They were alien in many ways. For instance, they hardly ever smiled.

"They probably will go when the young ones are old enough to travel," White Hare answered her father.

"It can't be soon enough to suit me." Goat Killer scowled. "We welcomed them and they guard their animals and their tent as if we would steal their possessions. I don't like their secretiveness, and I don't trust them."

White Hare remembered the day she went to collect Mara for a gathering trip to the beach. Inside the tent, Toacoatl was talking to her in a harsh, angry voice. Mara came out of the tent trying to hide the tears. No. White Hare did not like the southern men either.

Now, the young women sitting in front of Pink Shell's house saw the men tie on the poles that would become a travois to the sides of their mounts. Their bows were on their shoulders and their quivers hung from their hips.

"They're going hunting," Yellow Flower said. "it must be so easy to hunt with a horse. The hunter can see the game from far off. He can run like the wind. On a horse, you can carry home the kill without even getting out of breath."

Red Antler sauntered over to the young women. He had been visiting elsewhere. Now, he watched intently as the men on the horses disappeared down the trail. He followed up on Yellow Flower's thought.

"If it was any easier, we could whistle and an antelope would come running, skin itself, and crawl on the spit over the fire to roast. I wouldn't mind having one of those animals."

"Horses are bad." Everyone turned to look at Mara.

"What do you mean?" White Hare asked.

"They make bad things." She said a word in her own language. For as long as Mara had been living on the fringes of Chumash society, no Chumash word had been spoken that meant "war." She may have wondered if they even had such a word and envied them their peaceful existence. "Fighting," she said finally.

"Slaves." The others tried to make sense of her words. What were slaves? "Bad people come on horses."

"What does she mean?" They were still discussing it when Mara looked at the sun.

"Late," she said. "We go now." She motioned to Sena and Rasha. They rose and the three women walked swiftly down the hill.

Confrontation

Summer solstice was almost upon them. Already, Black Raven was keeping his vigils in the condor cave. A team of antap, sleeping in relays, made sure to awaken him in time to see how close the sun's first ray was to the rock painting on the wall. As soon as the ray and the condor in the painting met, it was time to proclaim the year's center.

Black Raven was not the only one who was busy. All the rock art had to be renewed. Antap and initiates prepared the sacred paint. They pounded rock of various colors and mixed it with rabbit fat until it was the right consistency. Only they knew all the locations of the sacred paintings. They carried their paint in specially prepared baskets. The rock art told the relationships of the stars and the creatures who lived in the heavens.

Celebrations honoring the sun and the sky and Mother Earth were being held in every village and town in the Chumash territories. It was a time for visiting and rejoicing with the young people who had just gained their status as adults in the community. Yellow Flower was going to be honored at the dancing this year. White Hare and her parents visited the graves of all her grandparents and great-grandparents. Father's parents were buried at the cemetary at Satwiwa, of course, but she had visited their graves the last time she was there and had laid flowers over their burial mounds.

During the year, condor, eagle and hawk feathers were gathered to tie onto the solstice pole in the center of the dancing circle. For the dancing, some of the people dressed as animals. White Hare's spirits were light as she prepared for the day. She wanted to ask Dancing Bear if he would dance with her on the night of Solstice Day, but it was not easy to find just the right moment. She was afraid someone else might have asked him already. Perhaps Otter Girl had, and he would reject White Hare. He would do it kindly, of course. After all, it was she who had insisted that their friendship was only that and nothing more. She had no right to expect him to wait for her. She decided it was not of major importance. If all seemed right, she would ask. If not, it was not meant to be.

It was only a few days before the holiday when Mara came alone to visit White Hare. The day's work was done. Except for her accent, Mara could have passed for a young women of the Chumash. White Hare suggested they walk to Pink Shell's house, where her friends usually gathered in the evenings.

Yellow Flower was already there. "Your husband makes you work too hard," Yellow Flower said. "You never have enough time for visiting and fun. You should tell him to do more things for himself."

"Husband?" Mara repeated the word as if she did not know what Yellow Flower was talking about. But Mara's memory was sharp, and White Hare was sure she had told her that word.

"Husband," she reminded her. "Like Red Antler is to Pink Shell. Like my mother and father."

Mara shook her head vehemently. "Toacoatl is not a husband to me."

Even Pink Shell, who didn't talk as much as Yellow Flower, wanted to know. "Then why do you serve him and do his work for him?" White Hare waited for the answer too.

When Mara did not speak at once, White Hare prompted her.

"If he's not your husband, what is he to you?"

"Master."

It was a word of Mara's language. It was not one she knew a Chumash word for. The others looked at one another in puzzlement.

Mara tried to explain. "He paid cocoa beans for me. I was captured from another people. Mara and Sena and I are not Aztec, we are Toltec. Slaves."

It was another foreign word.

"I am like his bow and quiver of arrows. Like his blankets."

No one knew what to say. White Hare felt a dawning of understanding at last. She took Mara by the shoulders and held her tightly. "That can't be," she said. "No one belongs to someone else that way."

"In the place where we lived, it can be," Mara said simply.

That she accepted her condition was more than White Hare could take. "You aren't in his country anymore. You're here now. Don't go back when he goes. Stay with us."

Mara breathed deeply. It was more like sighing. "I thank you for what you say. . . ." She hesitated.

"You will stay here, won't you?" Pink Shell asked. "Grey Eagle and Black Raven and everyone will protect you. "Families here will adopt you and the others if they want to stay. Just tell Toacoatl you don't want to be with him anymore." She clapped her hands as if that was the end of it.

Mara laughed as if she had heard a very funny joke, but her eyes were not laughing. "Toacoatl is very strong," she said. "I will not cause trouble for my friends." It was all she would say on the subject.

White Hare was not satisfied with her answer. She told her mother about the conversation later.

"Are you sure she used the right words?" Blue Star asked. "To own someone like a thing, to pay for them like a pot or a cup—I have never heard of such a custom."

"They own the horses, don't they?" White Hare countered. "She said more things that are even more terrible. She said during the holidays in the place where she lived, people hunt children and kill them to give their gods."

"With arrows and spears?" Blue Star asked incredulously. "That can't be what she meant. She doesn't know our words well enough. She must be saying the wrong word about owning. What does the word *master* mean anyway? It's not a word I know."

"I told her that if he treats her badly, she should stay with us. Did I do right?"

"A husband who is cruel to his wife can be brought

to trial among us. If he's judged guilty by the antap council, she can go back to her family's keesh and he must pay them restitution. The foreigners don't live under our laws, and *slave* and *master* are foreign words. But if he treats her cruelly, I don't see why she should tolerate it.

"I think Gray Eagle and the council will permit her and the women to stay if that is their wish, but they won't fight the foreign men if they insist on keeping them. Mara said something about money buying them. Black Raven has the most money in the village. Maybe he can buy them away from Toacoatl," Blue Star suggested.

"I don't know if he would sell them. They would have to do their own work then. They act as if they're too important to work."

Blue Star could see that her daughter was upset. "It may be best if we didn't interfere," she warned her. "It might cause trouble."

"These aren't rabbits, Mother." White Hare knew Blue Star had never forgotten what happened three years ago before. She still wondered, though, if she could have acted differently in the same circumstances.

"I don't want to cause trouble either. That is what Mara said, that it would cause trouble if she told him she decided to stay with us when he and the men moved on. Maybe I could just tell Toacoatl that it's wrong to be cruel. It doesn't matter that he's an important man where he comes from. Gray Eagle is important, and he's never cruel. He cares for all of us the way a leader should. Black Raven is good to his wives." White Hare's voice grew strained as she tried to keep it under control.

Blue Star saw that her daughter would not rest until she did all she could to correct the situation so her friends could be happy. It brought back to her the last words her father communicated to her as he lay dying. She wondered, as she looked at her daughter, if she also had the gift. If she could hear the voice of a spirit or a dying soul, it was a private thing. Blue Star could not discuss it with her unless and until she began to ask questions.

White Hare might be asking herself those questions, but unless she asked, she would have to find the answers herself. It was part of what Blue Star's father said. White Hare had to go on a quest, and she had to deal with the events in her own way. It was to be part of her growing up and gaining the confidence she needed. Blue Star's father had sight. It was a thing Blue Star did not comprehend completely. Her gift was not as strong as her father's, but White Hare's might be. All Blue Star could do was hope that she would ask so that Blue Star could guide her to the best of her ability.

"If you must try to speak to Toacoatl, I suppose you must," Blue Star said. "Just try to remember that their customs are different and try not to let your words offend."

White Hare walked down to the foreign encampment. She walked slowly, hesitantly, rehearsing in her mind what she might say. She reminded herself, so that she could not forget, that Toacoatl was their wot, the leader. She must not offend his dignity and make things worse for the women. She would make sure to speak very respectfully, as if she were talking to Gray Eagle. She had quite a bit of his language, but she had to think to make sure she put the words together the right way.

She finally stood outside the foreign tent. It was large, large enough indeed for all seventeen of them. Many skins had gone into its making. She walked to the tent flap and called out, "I am White Hare. May I enter?"

Toacoatl's brother came to the opening. He did not speak to her. "I came to talk with Toacoatl," she said in the foreign language as she believed Mara would have said it, with great respect. She hoped her voice did not tremble.

The boy motioned for her to come inside. Toacoatl walked up to them. It was evident that he had been studying Hokan when he said, "What do you want?" very clearly in her own language.

As she did when she spoke to Mara beyond her knowledge of the southern language, she used words of both languages and included gestures. It did not take her long to realize that her rehearsed speech was worthless. She could see his eyes become hard and his mouth form an impatient line as she spoke. The language barrier was only part of the problem, she realized. Her pleas and arguments made no sense to him because he did not think he was cruel. To him, his way was right. Hers were the attitudes that were foreign. She resolved that since she had come this far, she would say what she had to anyway. She concluded with, "I ask you to be kinder to your women."

When she was finished, Toacoatl said with barely supressed anger, "You speak too much with Mara. Do not speak to my women again. Women are for work and for making babies, not for telling men how to behave. Tell them no more about Chumash ways. Do not come back."

White Hare turned away from him sadly and began climbing the path back toward the village. Her effort was more than wasted. Now, she could incur his wrath if she even talked to her friends again. Tears of frustration stung her eyes. Her mind was so much on what had just transpired that she barely saw Dancing Bear standing on the trail until she was almost upon him.

She had just about made up her mind to ask Dancing Bear to be with her the night of summer solstice, but all thoughts about the holiday were driven from her mind now. With the tears in her eyes and her face burning from the confrontation with Toacoatl, she could not even speak. She turned away from Dancing Bear and lowered her eyes.

He had to see that she was much too disturbed about something to try to engage her in conversation. If she had to talk at all now, she was sure to burst into uncontrollable sobs like a baby. When she looked again, he was striding away swiftly. She tried to swallow down the lump that burned her throat and made it hard to breathe.

She did not go back to the village. Even if her mother was wise enough not to ask, the answer was right there on her face—failure. White Hare wanted nothing so much as to be alone. She wandered toward the other side of the hill away from home and questions. Not very far away the hill ended abruptly in a sheer forty-foot drop. In spite of her inner turmoil, she walked carefully, keeping well away from the edge.

A sound made White Hare turn in time to see one of the foals running up the hill. It must have escaped the corral. Toacoatl and his men were running after it. The foal cried fearfully at being away from his mother. He was confused. He did not know the way back to her. The cries of the men increased his terror. One of them opened the gate to the corral, probably intending to catch the colt mounted on one of the other horses.

White Hare looked down to see all of the horses running loose amid frantic running and screaming. The colt was running toward her. No—not toward her, but toward the edge of the cliff.

She knew that of all her friends, she was the one most afraid of the large animals. The men of the village and the curious youngsters wanted to study the creatures, but except for the birth of the first foal, the Aztecs never allowed them near. The other two had been born during the deepest part of the night and were already nursing when the villagers awoke. The southerners signed to the Chumash to stay away, that the horses were tame only for them, that they would bite and stamp anyone else.

White Hare believed it. She had never tried to go near the horses. Even when she walked to the encampment, she always gave the corral a wide margin, but the baby was going to fall over the edge and be killed on the rocks below unless she did something.

She ran toward the colt. He saw her and swerved even closer to the cliff. She could never catch him in time. "Oh, Mother," she called out as she ran. It was not Blue Star she called, but Chupu, the All Mother. "Don't let him die."

Perhaps it was because she never prayed for herself. Perhaps it happened because it would have in any case, but the colt's hooves became tangled in the wild cucumber vines that grew profusely at the edge of the hill. He sprawled out, caught but unharmed, and cried piteously. She was fast; that was the reason for her name. She rushed to him and knelt by his side to hold and comfort him while she worked to unravel the vines from his legs. He got to his feet, but did not move. Her arms still around him firmly, she wondered if she could turn him around and lead him back.

Then she felt the ground tremble. The mares and the stallion screamed in their loud, trumpetlike voices as they rushed toward her and the colt. The Aztecs were behind them and the whole village was running behind the them. Amid the yells and the cries were the voices of her father and mother shouting her name.

The world seemed to be rushing toward her. She felt she was about to be engulfed. She knew for a certainty that the terrible animals were going to crush the life out of her for daring to lay a hand on one of them.

Her only hope lay in the colt. If she was close enough, they might fear to harm their baby. She lay her head and shoulders over its back, eyes shut, holding tight. She heard an intake of breath from hundreds of mouths and braced herself. Nothing happened. She thought for half a moment that she felt warmth and softness.

Then a loud scream filled the air. She lifted her head and opened her eyes to see Toacoatl holding the stallion by his rope as the powerful animal reared angrily, its eyes blazing. The mares were also straining at the ropes thrown over their necks. It took the strength of all the men to pull them back. In spite of Toacoatl's anger, he had saved her. If she could only find her voice. She wanted to thank him, but she could not speak.

Toacoatl's brother began to lead the first colt back to the corral. Two other men took the other young ones. Then four of the men leaped to the backs of their horses. It was an awesome sight, the four men mounted all at once. The villagers hung back.

Toacoatl brought the stallion back to where White Hare stood on the edge of the cliff.

"Next time," he said, "they will kill you." Then he wheeled around and drove his mount down the hill.

For a moment White Hare was too stunned to do anything. It occurred to her that she understood him even though he spoke in his own language.

The next moment, the villagers were upon her, feeling her for bruises, looking for blood. There was no scratch. Blue Star reached her and held her tightly. The others backed away as Black Raven and Gray Eagle came forward.

"Is the maiden safe?" Black Raven asked. He stood in dignity, holding his carved, eagle-headed staff.

"She has suffered no harm," Blue Star answered for her. White Hare hid her face in her mother's hair and sobbed.

"I was only trying to help," she whispered weakly.

"I know," Blue Star answered.

Blue Star and Goat Killer led her back to their keesh. She saw Dancing Bear as the crowd separated to allow the small family to walk through. He seemed concerned, questioning. If only he had looked at her that way when she had first emerged from Toacoatl's tent, she might have spoken to him. Now, she only wanted to go home and cry herself to sleep like a little girl.

She felt much too young even to think of speaking to Dancing Bear. She turned away and let her parents lead her home.

Solstice Day

The village was assembled again on the ridge behind the village. White Hare was with them, standing between her parents. The grey sky grew lighter as they watched solemnly. Clouds reflected the sun's rays from below the horizon, making gold and scarlet ribbons to decorate the mountains. The moon grew pale and the last of the stars winked out as the sun rose on the morning of Summer Solstice Day.

No one spoke. The babies were quieted and the small children hushed as the sun emerged from behind the northeastern mountains. Black Raven, in all his finest paint and feathers, lit the white sage leaves in an abalone shell with a taper from the sacred antap fire. He breathed in the smoke first, then he held it out over the earth. Even on the day of the sun, Earth, who gave life to all her children, must be honored first. Then he held the bowl toward the rising sun where it was wreathed in its glory of shining clouds. Black Raven and the priests said the holy words in the sacred antap tongue, the ancient first language. Two more times they chanted the blessings while Black Raven pointed the bowl to the two holy mountains.

Finally he held the bowl out toward the People. The morning breeze blew the scent to where they stood. Friends and families embraced. White Hare grasped her mother and her father lovingly. She knew how much she meant to them. After years of childlessness, their special prayers to the Earth Mother were answered when Blue Star gave birth to a healthy girl. Now, even though her own escapades sometimes bothered her afterward when she was calm enough to think over her actions, her parents never rebuked her. They accepted her with her impulsiveness, her running away and coming home late with no more than a grateful sigh. None of her friends' parents were really strict, but she felt especially lucky.

Yellow Flower and Pink Shell came over to embrace White Hare's family. She followed them to their parents. "A good and fruitful year to all of us," she said as she greeted everyone she encountered. It was a beautiful day, but White Hare felt that a cloud still hung over her.

Mats with food were brought out and set up in the village center. White Hare took a bowl of acorn mush and currants when someone handed it to her, but she ate absentmindedly.

"There are going to be stories and animals dances all morning until nap time," Pink Shell reminded White Hare. "You'll stay with us, won't you?"

White Hare knew Pink Shell was trying to be kind. Dancing Bear was not far away, eating with his friends. She was not ready to put the incident of the horses behind her.

"I don't think I feel all that well," she said. "Please excuse me. I might be back later."

"Oh, you're not sick, are you?" Yellow Flower, asked pouting. "The new adult dance will happen when the shadows grow long. You can't miss that. I'm an adult for the first time on a Summer Solstice Day. You have to be there to watch me dance."

"Then I must rest now so I can be there later," White Hare said. She turned away.

Ever since her confrontation with Toacoatl, she had been subdued. Her bright smile no longer came so easily and her step was hesitant. Following her intution had gotten her into trouble one time too many. Now, she was less sure of herself.

Again and again, she went over in her mind what had happened to her two days ago. It seemed to her that there was something important that she missed somehow, but she could not imagine what it could be.

White Hare walked into her quiet keesh and plopped herself on top of her sleeping robe. It was too late now to speak to Dancing Bear about tonight, even if she wanted to. He would probably be with Otter Girl. It did not matter. Pink Shell and Yellow Flower and all her other friends could grow up and find their destined mates. She was never going to grow up, really grow up and have the wisdom to think before speaking and making a fool of herself, wisdom to think before acting and so cause trouble for her friends.

"I wish I could die," she muttered to herself. She covered herself up with her furs to lie alone with her thoughts in the dark.

Memories of other Summer Solstice Days came rushing back to her, days when she was happy. Even the

Summer Solstice Days after Grandfather's death had left her with a happy memory, because all the mourners walked together in a holy circle around the dance floor to the chants of condolence from the rest of the village. She always knew her people were with her, and that they were one in joy and sorrow. Some days stood out like bright crystals of quartz among dull stones.

The Summer Solstice Day, when she was thirteen, was a very special day for her. It was the first one after she had been to the Women's Lodge. The morning of her initiation into adulthood was a day she could never forget.

The day before summer solstice, the boys were brought to one of the sacred caves and the girls were brought to another. For a whole day, they had nothing to eat and only spring water to drink so their bodies would contain no impurities. People who had undergone initiation were not permitted to speak of it except to antap priests, so the proceedings sparked much curiosity for most of the girls in White Hare's group. A few were really frightened.

No one was forced to participate, but certain adult privileges were withheld from any young person who did not. White Hare was too curious to want to miss it.

The girls in White Hare's age group sat in a circle around the priestess. There were markings on the cave walls of the sun and stars and animals. In spite of her fear of the unknown, White Hare was exhilarated. Something very special was about to happen and afterward, she would never be quite the same.

The priestess explained. "I will give each of you a potion to drink made from the sacred datura plant. Ever since Momoy, one of the Daughters of the Earth, discovered its uses and taught them to the antap priests, this has been the way for our children to be brought into adulthood. After you drink, you will dance. Soon you will be sleepy. We will take you to a place where you can lie down. During your rest, you will see things differently. Some of what you see may confuse you, but try to remember it. Everything has a meaning. A spirit may talk to you. Whether it is in human or animal form, you must try to remember what it says.

"Tomorrow or the next day, one of us will talk to you privately to help you sort out your thoughts and feelings about your vision. We will be guarding you so, don't be afraid. Remember, there will be something to follow to show you the way back in case you go too far in your vision."

The datura potion was poured out of the basket and into a stone bowl. Each girl came forward to kneel in front of the bowl and drink. White Hare only took a few swallows before the priestess lifted her head and invited the next girl to come forward.

The priestesses chanted their songs; one of their helpers shook a rattle while the other blew on a small bone flute. It was not a dance with learned steps. White Hare swayed to the music. As it became faster, she lifted her feet and set them down and turned in time to the beat of the rattle. The other girls danced around her and the fire threw their shadows up on the walls. It was easy to feel there were spirits among them.

She danced until she began to feel dizzy. One of the helpers escorted her to a mat on the side of the cave and helped her to be comfortable. "Rest now," she said.

White Hare felt warm and sleepy at first. She could

still hear the music and the stamps of the girls as they danced. Then, she found herself feeling quite awake and startled to see that the cave's gray walls were glowing blue. She knew they were not very far inside, but only dim light entered the cave from outside. She stood up to inspect the cave wall. It felt smooth now, unlike the rough stone it was before.

She turned toward the dancers to see the last of the girls led away to rest within the confines of the cave. Not far from where she stood, two priestesses and two volunteers sat and watched over the initiates. The younger priestess pointed and both of the volunteers went immediately over to one of the girls who was shaking violently. Their backs were toward White Hare. She could only see how they straightened the girl's limbs and held her head so she could not harm herself on the floor of the cave.

The girl finally lay still and they left her to attend another. White Hare looked to see which one of the girls they were helping. She saw herself.

"Holy Mother! she exclaimed.

White Hare remembered her experience very clearly. She remembered also that she had the power to rise into the air in her vision. It was quite amazing to float above the village. She saw what everyone was doing. There was Pink Shell's grandmother pounding acorn meal; there was Yellow Hare's little sister weaving flowers into the reeds that covered her keesh. She looked toward her own home and saw her parents through the walls! They were sitting on the floor with their eyes closed and their expressions very solemn. They might be praying for her right now. It did not seem right to watch them. She floated away.

White Hare wondered how high she could go. She went up and up until she saw eagles nesting and could look into the eyes of a soaring condor. It made her dizzy to look down. She was even with the mountain peaks. She did not enjoy being quite so high even though she could not fall and she knew her body was safe and being guarded back at the cave.

She floated back down until she was just above the chaparral. How vast everything looked from the mountaintops, though. She kept just above the chaparral and followed the trail to the sea. It was more fun to hover close enough to see the world again.

She stopped to admire a flower. A hummingbird dipped her long beak into the heart of the flower to sip its nectar. White Hare moved herself into the hummingbird and tasted the nectar with her. The world was too wonderful to be believed. She wanted to see and taste it all.

She moved out of the hummingbird and followed a gray coyote. She watched how he stalked a green lizard sunning itself on a rock. Before the lizard knew a thing, it was in the coyote's mouth. White Hare decided not to enter the coyote to taste his dinner with him, but she watched. As an experiment, she touched his fur. He did nothing to indicate that he felt her. She had no substance here, but she became curious about this as well. She exerted all her will and reached out and pulled one of his ears. He jumped. He could see and smell nothing, but he was startled just the same. Then he went back to his meal. It was not her body that he felt. She knew that was still in the cave. It was her will. She could do things! She could make herself felt if her

will was strong enough! It was an exciting thought. Again, she reached out and pulled, exerting all her will in her mind, as hard as she could.

With a yelp and a yip-yip, the coyote ran into the underbrush with what was left of the lizard hanging out of his mouth as if a ghost was after him, White Hare laughed with delight. This was fun.

She continued following the path until she came down to the beach. This was supposed to be a serious quest and so far she was wasting time testing the boundaries of her powers during a datura vision. Antap might enter the trance state as often as they felt it was necessary, but this very likely was going to be her only experience with it. What else did she want to know or to try?

The priestess said she might be able to talk to a spirit. That was something to think about. She began to float out over the ocean as she considered it. Why stay in once place when there was so much to see?

There were Sky Coyote and Sky Bear, of course. The boys liked Sky Coyote. There were so many funny stories about him. It was said that he like to tease girls. Well, she had just teased one of his kind and she felt good about it. It might be best to avoid him. She knew very little about Sky Bear and most of the others. Sun and his daughters with their skirts made of live rattlesnakes were interesting, but she certainly did not want to meet them. They had a mountain of bones from the people they ate piled up in front of their crystal house. It was said that they especially liked to eat children.

Of her family, she barely remembered three of her grandparents. Mother's father was different. He always felt close. She wondered if he was not hovering close to her sometimes. "Grandfather," she called. "Are you here?"

There was no answer. He said she could call him if she ever needed him. She did not need him now. She was having a wonderful time exploring.

White Hare remembered an older girl telling her that the ocean went on forever after the islands. She wondered now if that was true or if it was only a tale told to children. Maybe she could find out. She floated past them. She saw their villages and the people in them. Even here, the People were getting ready for Summer Solstice Day and the new initiates were having their visions. She knew there were other countries, Navajo and Hopi to the east and the Salmon Eaters to the far north, but even these islands were populated by Chumash families. She saw the waves pounding their beaches. Then, she looked out over the sea.

She saw nothing but the blue expanse. Sea gulls flew by calling to each other. Sea otters played and walruses hunted. Giant fish swam under the ocean. Dolphins leaped shining in the sunlight, looking bluer than the water that fell from them. If there was anything else in the world after the ocean, it was too far away to worry about.

The sun was out here too. The day must be getting old. If she continued on her course, she would be going right toward him. She stopped and looked back. There, so far away that it looked like a brown and green discoloration floating between the blue water and the blue sky, was home.

A silver streak that she could not feel extended across the water. This must be the guide that would lead her back to her body in the cave. How clever the priestesses were to arrange it. She floated back, swifter than an eagle, faster than the wind.

Most of the other girls were already yawning and walking around. The older priestess was kneeling over her and looking into one of her eyes, which she held open with two of her fingers. Then White Hare yawned also, and stretched. She felt as if she had woken up from a happy dream.

"Here I am," she said. The woman's expression was a stern one.

"You were very far away," she said. "Was a spirit talking to you? Did you feel it was rude to leave? We were beginning to worry."

"Sorry," White Hare mumbled. "I couldn't find anyone to talk to. I was just exploring. There was so much to see, I forgot how late it was."

The priestess looked at her sideways. "You mean you conducted your own experience? You decided what to do and see?"

"Isn't it that way with everyone?" White Hare asked. She hoped she hadn't done anything wrong.

"It is a little unusual," the woman admitted. "Understanding the meaning of your vision will take some thinking."

The girls were given water and a small meal before they were brought back to the village. The next day was Summer Solstice Day. White Hare felt so energized by her experience, she wanted to dance all night.

Later, during her interview, she learned that many of her age-mates were taken by their spirit guides and shown their future. Some found they had the gift of remembering healing plants and how to prepare them.

Others learned that hunting or fishing or boat building was the skill to pursue. Still others discovered a knack for tool making or carving or trading. The priestesses did not know what to make of White Hare's vision.

"Tell me," the oldest antap woman said to her, "did you learn anything at all that made you understand yourself better?"

"Well," White Hare said, as seriously and honestly as she could, "I learned that the world is very big and that I'm curious about it. And I learned that I like to have fun." She smiled as she remembered the trick she played on the coyote. "Maybe my vision was trying to show me that I have a long way to go before I can know myself. There is so much in life that's interesting."

"Have you ever thought you would want to be antap?" It was a question White Hare had never expected to hear. She knew that not everyone in the elite group was born to it. Some were adopted into the priesthood.

"No. I couldn't. It's not for me. No," White Hare shook her head. She wasn't sure why she felt so strongly about it. Perhaps it had something to do with her grandfather.

"You have your own path, then. Follow it carefully." The old priestess spoke gently with encouragement in her voice. For some reason, it gave White Hare a little chill, though. Her own path. It was something to think about.

White Hare pulled her fur cover away when she heard voices coming from outside. The sun was very bright as it streamed through the smoke hole above her. People were wishing each other a good rest as they retired for the warmest part of the day. Blue Star and Goat

Killer were just outside saying good-bye to their friends.

"Are you all right?" Blue Star said as soon as she saw White Hare on the bed. "Do you feel hot all over? Is your belly hurting?" White Hare felt ashamed for making her worry. She was perfectly all right. "There's nothing wrong," she assured her parents. "I'm going to go out now. I'll see you later." They probably wanted to be alone. She was getting tired of moping, anyway. She had a healthy young body and plenty of energy. It was impossible to stay cooped up on this beautiful Summer Solstice Day.

White Hare wandered toward a field not far away where she heard someone drumming on a hollow log and rattles and someone playing a lively melody on a bone flute.

The long grass was pressed down all around and a score of children were assembled in the shadow of a large oak tree. Brown Bear, Dancing Bear's father, was doing the Bear Dance. The children laughed and pretended to be frightened every time he lunged at them. He wore a bear skin, and the claws dangled down by his arms. He stretched them out as if he was trying to get the children in a deadly bear hug.

It was seldom that anyone happened on a real bear, but now and then someone did. In spite of their laughter, the children were being taught that bears were dangerous and not to be teased. A bear's embrace could kill; its huge claws could tear a child or even an adult apart. Brown Bear had killed the bear whose coat he wore, but he did not go out looking for it. He found it by accident and was very lucky to get away with his life. He was already within its grasp when he was able to get a flint knife between its ribs and kill it first. In doing so, he won his name when he was a young man.

White Hare sat next to Goat and Climber, the nine-year-old twins. The oldest here were only ten or eleven summers old. She clapped and whistled along, enjoying the show. She felt almost her usual, cheerful self again.

Suddenly, another bear sprang onto the scene from behind the tree. Brown Bear pretended to fight with him and the children laughed as the two "bears" rolled on the ground. The "older bear" began to squeal as the younger one trounced him soundly. He ran away squealing, and the children laughed as Dancing Bear (she could see now that it was he) stood and made growling noises. He must have arranged all this earlier with his father so the older man could rest from dancing in the heat.

The man who was striking the hollow log began to tell a story, which Dancing Bear proceeded to act out.

"The young bear is enjoying his victory." Dancing Bear strutted around, making faces. He saw White Hare in the group and looked startled for a moment. Then he grinned at her.

"But he is hungry." Dancing Bear frowned. "So he looks for something good to eat." Dancing Bear looked high and low, in the children's ears and under their feet. The children were rolling on the ground laughing by now.

"Then, he finds berries." The children sat still again to watch as Dancing Bear pretended to stuff berries in his mouth.

"But the berries have been there too long. They were fermented and the bear has been made very drunk."

In between talking, the drummer drummed his log for sound effects. By now, Dancing Bear was staggering about and scratching his head, wondering why he was bumping into things. At last, he lay on his back with his feet in the air while White Hare and the children laughed until they cried.

The drummer concluded the narration. "Even drunk bears must be avoided, no matter how funny they look."

The flutist played the final notes and the rattler gave his instrument a final shake. All the children rushed over to Dancing Bear to poke and tickle him. He sat up and grabbed a few, wrestling with them and laughing too.

White Hare walked away. She was too old to wrestle with her friend like one of the children. Perhaps she could find someone who needed help with something. She heard running steps behind her and turned in time to see Dancing Bear cover the final distance that separated them. His face was painted, and he had fur stuck on all over his body with sticky sap.

"Did you like it?" he asked.

She couldn't help smiling. "It was very good. Dancing Bear is really a dancing bear."

"Will I see you at the fire tonight?" The change of subject startled her.

She felt herself growing suddenly shy. The other day he walked away from her just when she most needed him, no, just when she needed someone to be sympathetic after Toacoatl's harsh words. Dancing Bear was like that. He sometimes seemed to be angry for no reason at all. It kept her off balance. She hesitated while she thought.

"You haven't asked someone else?" he asked, when she still said nothing.

"No." She looked down at his feet to see if they had fur stuck to them, too. It was hard to look up.

"I haven't either. It won't hurt you only to dance with an old friend, will it?"

Again she remembered something. He had looked as if he wanted to speak to her when her parents led her down the hill. He might have been ashamed of his earlier rudeness. She suspected that there was something that needed to be said between them and every time an opportunity came close, one or the other of them could not speak. Some day, perhaps, they might find a way to say those things—unless of course, she was imagining something that was not there.

"I'll be at the dancing," she murmured very softly.

"I have to go wash," he said and he turned to run toward the stream before she could be sure how much meaning there was behind his invitation.

Solstice Night

W hite Hare felt better after Dancing Bear spoke to her. She went to the village square to help herself to something to eat. Both smoked meat and fresh were available in abundance. The Aztecs had contributed several freshly slain deer. Meat was always a welcome relief from the constant diet of fish and seafood, and she was glad to have it.

She wondered whether the southern men would come up the hill to join in the celebration and if she would be embarrassed if they did. She wondered what she would do if the women came with them. Since Toacoatl had told her not to speak to his women, she'd only seen them from a distance. The three worked together gathering roots and seeds, fetching and cooking, skinning, tanning and sewing.

She scooped up some of the meat along with cooked bulbs and roots into a simple eating basket. After she finished, she went back for more, this time stew flavored with onions and carrots. The smoked filets of fish smelled so tantalizing, she took a few of those, too,

with some watercress and tender, green, delicately flavored leaves. She went back for walnuts saved from
last year and new berries for dessert. A few old men
and women were sitting near the food baskets gossip-
ing and lazily brushing away the flies.

She finished her food and patted her tummy. It was
a long while since she had eaten so much at one meal.
If she ate like this too often, she would soon begin to
resemble Pink Shell's mother. The thought made her
smile.

She went to wash off her greasy hands and face at
the stream. Mara was there, filling a pot with water.
She saw White Hare and smiled to her, but she bent
to her task and said nothing. As she bent over the water,
White Hare saw welts on her back. Anger flooded
through her. She felt she had to say something. Before
she spoke, however, it occured to her that it was her
interference that had created further cruelty in the foreign prince (if that was what he was) in the first place.
She fought down her impulse and did not speak.

The shadows were growing long when the people
assembled for the dancing. Most of the villagers spent
the afternoon napping or taking leisurely walks to enjoy the beauty the Earth gives to her children. Now
they were refreshed, and several hundred people milled
around the dancing area. White Hare stayed near the
outer fringes of the crowd and watched while Black
Raven and the twelve consecrated antap priests and
priestesses made their circles, chanting and purifying
the area around the Solstice pole.

First, the mourners entered the circle. The women
walked in the center, closest to the decorated, feathered
pole, and the men circled around them. They all had

shorn hair to signify the loss of a loved one. The women in the middle cried and the men moaned and wailed as they walked in the death circle. Those around them sang songs of consolation, reminding them that every soul must make its death journey into the world of spirits.

After the mourners' dance, the area was purified again of its sadness and the new young men and women danced to celebrate their initiation.

Yellow Flower walked into the circle with the rest. She wore her long ceremonial reed skirt and a chain of canyon sunflowers around her neck. There were several in her hair also. Her eyes were still glowing with her special experience, the aftermath of her day in the cave. The new adults walked proudly and with grace as the villagers cheered them and sang welcoming songs. Music accompanied their twists and turns.

Everyone had his or her own special experience to remember and relive during the dance. Three years ago, when it was her turn to dance, Pink Shell who was then still Long Eye, had worn shells around her neck and woven into her hair. White Hare found pink quartz to tie on a leather cord around her neck when it was her turn. She saw her mother and father and all of their generation watching wistfully. Even crones and bent-over old men clutching canes pounded their sticks in time to the music.

The welcoming dance had meaning for all of them. It helped to blend the village into a cohesive unit. The People were like a living tree with roots that went down deep into the earth. New branches were as important to the tree's life as the roots were, because they reached out into the sunlight to make food while the roots drank the water. The old people were like the roots. Her parents' generation was the trunk, and the young people were the branches, soon to put forth new shoots and buds. These were the children and the babies. Even as the tree aged and grew, it stayed the same. White Hare liked her tree image. It felt good.

Yellow Flower's little brother and sister ran to her and she swung them in the air. It was like a signal. Everyone rushed out onto the dancing floor.

White Hare joined the twisting line as the rattles and flutes played faster. The sun was lowering in the south-western sky. Torches were lit around the dancing floor as the sky became purple, then violet, than black with hundreds of stars. The group was beginning to break into smaller circles as some of the new couples wandered off to be alone, when White Hare saw Dancing Bear walking toward her.

He wore a reed skirt as did all of them. His hair was plaited into two long braids that went down to his waistband. He wore a bear claw around his neck on a leather cord and two feathers tucked into a band on his forehead.

The torchlight reflected off his deeply tanned skin, exaggerating the rippling muscles of his chest and his legs as he walked. His jaw was strong and his eyes were sincere and steady. He was not wild and headstrong as were many of the young men of the village. In spite of the tension that sometimes flared between them, she had to admit that most of the time, he was like a tree to lean on when she was tired and a good companion when she wanted to run or only talk. She smiled now as he approached her and held out her two hands to him when a sudden cry made everyone turn and the music came to an abrupt halt.

The fourteen Aztec men stood together on the edge of the dancing floor. Four of them were mounted and all were armed. The people of the village, as one, moved back and Toacoatl, sitting proudly and arrogantly astride the black stallion, rode to the center of the floor and faced the villagers.

"Good Chumash people," Toacoalt said in Hokan, "your alchuklash, Black Raven, invited us to join you today. I hope you liked the meat we provided."

The people nodded and murmured thanks. Black Raven and Gray Eagle stood together in front of the villagers. How dare they come armed to a solstice celebration? Of course, they did not know the customs. White Hare felt a premonition of something evil in spite of the gracious words she heard. Mara must have taught him to speak so well. No wonder he kept her with him. And to think it was she who'd taught Mara.

"You worship a good goddess. We respect her also." Toacoatl nodded toward the solstice pole. It was piled high at its base with many flowers and seeds. "We have other gods, also," he continued. "Because you welcomed us, and because you are good people, we want to teach you about them. They can help you in many ways. They can give you strength and power and victory in war.

"First, we will do a dance in honor of our gods and then we will explain about them to you."

The Aztec men must have practiced when they were out on their hunts. They leaned forward to make the horses charge, then leaned to the side to make them turn. They grasped their mounts tightly between their knees and made the horses obey them.

One of the unmounted men put a figure made of branches and reeds in the shape of a man in the path of the horsemen. One by one they each rode past it and with a terrifying war cry, threw a spear into it. All four hit the center of the target. If they intended to show that one could fight well from the back of a horse, they proved it. But whom did they expect to fight? The Chumash had no enemies. All the towns and villages within a reasonable amount of travel were Chumash. A family did not fight itself. Even the Shoshoni and the Tongva were related by marriages. Individuals sometimes feuded, but real war? There had not been one for hundreds of years.

The riders lined up behind Toacoatl. "Because you are generous and have allowed us to live alongside your village, we wish to reward you. We will teach you about our gods. In three days' time, we will make a sacrifice. Then, you will understand the power of Aztec deities. You will become as we are. We will make warriors of your men.

"In two years, there will be two new mares ready to breed. Soon, we will have an army of mounted men on horses. I will lead you. We will conquer all the other villages and lead them to war in the south. There are bad people there who must be destroyed."

Gray Eagle faced him, and the People looked to their wot to speak for them. "My people have no argument with other Chumash towns. We do not make war with the Shoshoni or the Tongva who live near us without good reason. We have no desire to fight anyone. If you have arguments with other southerners, you must fight them without us."

The villagers began to mutter among themselves. A thing like this had never interrupted Solstice Day festivities.

"Listen to me, Simo'moans," Toacoatl said. "I am strong. I am a warrior. I have power and I have horses. You will learn to follow my gods and my ways. In three days, the sacrifice to my gods will take place. You will obey me."

He stared at Gray Eagle and at Black Raven, who stood at his side. Then, with their foot soldiers behind them, he and the others went slowly down the hill.

No one felt like dancing now. Gray Eagle walked to the solstice pole and held his hands out for silence. In olden days, before peace came to the People, he would have been their war leader, their captain.

"Do we want to fight for these Aztecs?" he asked the multitude before him.

"No!" The People shouted their answer in one great voice.

"Are we going to participate in a party for foreign gods and offend the Mother and the sun?"

"No!" they shouted again.

"If these southern strangers think they will force us to fight for them, they will have a war. It will be with us!"

White Hare had never seen her people like this. The celebration was over. There was loud speech and anger on every side. "What do they mean to do at this sacrifice?" was the question she heard on many lips. Dancing Bear had been swept from her side as the village reacted to the Aztec demands. Solstice Day was done.

She walked slowly to her keesh. From her bed, she heard Blue Star and Goat Killer discussing the situation into the night.

"We must drive them from our lands," Goat Killer said vehemently. "I knew they would make trouble."

"But our people will be killed in the fighting," Blue Star answered sadly. "Even if we do nothing, they will kill just to make their point unless we obey them. It frightens me. If only it was possible to reason with such people. Perhaps Black Raven can talk to them."

"The antap will always counsel peace. This time, it will not work. The Aztecs always have guards to warn them. If we could kill them while they sleep . . ."

"My husband! You would practice treachery?"

"To save our village, yes. Besides, after they desecrated our holiday, we owe them nothing. They were our guests, but they betrayed our trust."

"Shh. We must wait and see what the council decides. It is very late. You'll wake White Hare. Try to sleep now."

But White Hare was not sleeping. She was thinking. *She* was the one who had seen Toacoatl first on the beach more than two moons ago. *She* had offered the strangers hospitality. *She* was responsible. She began to think of what she might do if the Aztecs did not withdraw their demands.

Grandfather had said something long ago about vast distances. He said there were far places in the world. She strained to remember the exact words. Did he say she would see them? "Her own path." Those were words she had heard, both from her mother and from the antap. She hoped it did not mean she must go away with them to save her people, but if it would take that to avoid bloodshed, she would go and be grateful. She tried to imagine herself as another slave among cruel people. It was not a happy thought.

The next day over breakfast, no one spoke of anything else. The village was split into two camps. White Hare's father consulted with the other men. Hunters did not leave the village to hunt. Gatherers sat and talked. After the feast, supplies were getting low in the storage bins, but no one left the village. There was no clear course of action decided on concerning the Aztec's demands.

The antap invited all the village elders to come to a council. Afterward, Blue Star came to sit before Pink Shell's keesh where White Hare and her friends were waiting. The younger women sat silently, politely waiting until she was ready to speak.

"The council has decreed that for now, we will do nothing," Blue Star began. "They say they must investigate the strangers' gods more thoroughly. Their wot, Toacoatl, has some of our language, so Black Raven thinks he and a few of the other priests may be able to talk to them and reach some kind of compromise. They say they took readings from the stars and they do not see war, so the threat is not as urgent as it seems."

"This is all?" White Hare asked suddenly. "The strangers must be told they cannot force us to put other gods before Mother Earth."

"White Hare," her mother said a little sternly and a little sadly. "The antap rule us. They have led us wisely in spiritual matters for many generations. Chumash people have lived in these mountains since the Flood, when the gods first made people. Fourteen men, even with horses, can't make such a difference that we will no longer respect the decisions of our leaders."

"We never faced a threat like this one before," White Hare said impatiently. "We must not compromise. If we do, we will lose without a war. We have to oppose them. The antap are wrong! We will be destroyed if we follow their counsel."

"White Hare!" Blue Star could hardly speak. "I have allowed you too much freedom. I have never taught you disrespect. If you oppose our wise ones, you are no longer my daughter!"

"I'm sorry, Mother."

Everyone took a breath. They had never seen Blue Star angry before.

"I'm sorry, Mother," White Hare continued, "but the antap are wrong. We must oppose the Aztecs. If we can't drive them off, they will change us and we will lose the blessings of the Mother. I was warned that a threat would come to us from a faraway place. This is that threat. We must not compromise with them."

Her mother and her friends looked at her so strangely that she could no longer bear to stay with them. She had never opposed any adult, not even her own mother, in her life. Now, she was ready to stand against the entire antap cult. Her feelings possessed her more strongly than ever before. No matter what anyone thought or said, she must speak.

She knew she could not remain with them. Even as they stared at her in shock she rose and began to stroll through the village to find out how other people felt. She listened. Everywhere she walked she heard argument and confusion. Should the wot resolve the problem? *Could* Gray Eagle turn aside the threat? New gods to consider were an antap matter. Was the habit of listening to the antap so strong that there was no longer any choice?

White Hare did not want there to be a war. Her people would be hurt or killed. Her new friends who were servants to the Aztecs might be hurt. She, of all the villagers, understood the language of the strangers best. In negotiations, she could translate, but the sight of her would antagonize Toacoatl. Besides, there must be no negotiations. The strangers must leave. She only knew that in terms of the gods, there could be no compromise.

A short distance from the houses behind a growth of bushes and young trees, she heard deep voices. She went to look. One of the young men breathed in sharply. Then he saw she was alone. They were sharpening their knives and spearheads and affixing new arrow points and feathers to newly made, straightened stems. Dancing Bear was among them. He looked up as she walked over. "Do you think there's going to be fighting?" she asked timidly. Would they dare? she wondered to herself.

"We follow the antap rule," one of the boys said, bitterly.

"Then why are you preparing weapons?"

One of the younger boys laughed nervously.

"For hunting," Wolf said.

The others bent their heads over their tasks. Dancing Bear looked directly into her face.

"Just in case," he said softly.

Then Dancing Bear understood the danger too. Some were ready to fight, even though they were untrained in war. Some others were so opposed to fight-

ing the antap decision, they would struggle against
those who would defend them. There was going to be
a civil war. White Hare saw a picture in her mind of
Dancing Bear fighting bravely and leading the others
in the attack. Then, she saw him a moment later. There
was a spear protruding from his chest, his life's blood
staining the ground red. Her grandfather had special
sight. What if she had it too? What if what she saw
was not her imagination, but what was going to really
happen if there was war?

"No!" she shouted. The word lingered on the air in
the silence that followed. "What I mean is, I don't want
anyone to be hurt."

Dancing Bear's face became a mask, closed to her,
but there was dark anger in his eyes that she could not
mistake.

"In that case, you had better go warn your friends."
He turned away from her.

She walked away sadly. The day was almost over.
Unless something was done tomorrow to stop them,
the Aztecs would not wait. They were already helping
themselves to the contents of the storage bins. They
paraded on their horses to remind the villagers of their
power.

That night, there was no conversation in White
Hare's house. As she lay unsleeping under her rabbit-
skin blanket, her mind was at work devising a plan of
her own. If it were not for her, invaders would not be
besetting her village now. They would have passed by
on the beach.

Finally, she reached a decision. She made up her
mind to go down to the Aztec encampment at first light.

If she offered herself as a slave to them, they might take her and go away. If that was not enough to pacify them, she could offer herself to be their sacrifice. She was not quite sure of the meaning of that word yet, but she gathered it had something to do with dedicating a person to a god. She could continue to revere the Mother in her heart, even while learning to sing or dance or pray to a lesser god. Surely, the Mother would understand she was doing it for the sake of her people and forgive her.

Very early the next morning, before her mother and father awoke, she made her way down to the Aztec tent. The two guards were not standing nearby. Usually, one watched by the tent while the other circled the corral. The horses were still sleeping, facing in opposite directions and resting their heads on each other's backs. She kept far from them. She was not afraid they would alert the Aztecs. Her plan was to go directly to the entrance of the tent; in a moment they would know she was here. Only the fear of seeing the horses' huge eyes and big teeth made her move silently.

She heard the sound of men's voices talking within. The guards must have been called inside. Deciding it would be better to wait until they finished their conversation before she showed herself, she walked to the back of the enclosure. Then she sat, folding her knees in the dewy grass behind the tent to wait.

Toacoatl's voice drifted out to her. His speech of two nights ago must have been rehearsed. Even with his odd way of saying her words, she and the others had understood him. Now he spoke in his language. To her amazement, she heard the words and understood them clearly, as if the language he spoke was hers. She must have learned it better than she realized. Either that or the Mother was helping her.

"We'll sacrifice one warrior and two children to show them the proper ways to worship the gods."

White Hare froze. Now, she understood the entire meaning of the word. She almost forgot to breathe.

Toacoatl's brother spoke. "Even these gentle people will fight if you attempt such a thing."

"Then we must kill the children first so that when the men fight, we'll know how to choose our warrior. There are a fine pair of babies I noticed. They were born of the same mother and they look to be about a year old. The gods ought to be pleased with a sacrifice like that."

"No!" Mara screamed. They were talking about Pink Shell's children. White Hare clenched her hands. She was shaking like a blade of grass in the wind. She made herself keep still so they would not hear her.

She heard footsteps then, and a slap. "Woman, keep quiet!" It was Toacoatl's brother.

"I will not keep quiet. If your gods love you, why didn't they protect you from the colorless men with their gray shells and their terrible weapons?"

"At least we captured four of their runaway horses."

"Before you ran away yourself!" Mara's hate finally reached the surface.

"That's all she will say," Toacoatl's voice croaked. "Take her and put a gag in her mouth." White Hare heard the sound of struggling.

"You pretend you're a prince," Mara shouted as they dragged her to the far corner of the tent. White Hare was inches away from her now.

"You're a general who deserted his king and his troops and ran away with his friends and his slaves. You're nothing!" she spat.

"Tomorrow," Toacoatl answered in a terrible voice, "you will be the first to have your heart removed."

Mara started to scream. There was the sound of a heavy blow falling and the scream ended abruptly. White Hare heard Sena and Rasha moaning and crying.

"More noise out of you two," Toacoatl said harshly to the other women, "and you'll be silenced also." Their sobs tapered into gulps and heavy breathing. "Now we can plan," he continued to his men.

White Hare backed away. She was helpless. Her plan was the plan of a child who thinks she can matter enough to make a difference. Tomorrow was going to come, and there was nothing she could do about it.

The Aztecs wanted to sacrifice Pink Shell and Red Antler's baby boys. They wanted to sacrifice a warrior. Just as she felt responsible, Dancing Bear also had shared in the decision to bring the foreigners to their mountain. He would be the first to throw himself to his enemies and he would be the first to die.

Vision

The threat of death and violence in her beloved mountains caused White Hare's face to burn in hot waves of rage as she backed away. She was meant to hear this or fate would not have given her the power to understand the foreign words or guided her to this spot to hear them. She wandered along, hardly aware of where she was going as she pictured slain children, family and friends lying in pain and blood while the victorious war cries of the foreigners filled the air.

She found herself on a seldom-used trail near the stream. There were caves further up into the slopes. She walked downstream now, much farther than she had been in many years. She remembered that this stream led to a small pond bordered three-quarters of the way around by steep rock cliffs. She continued walking. The pond became a destination for her, a place to sit and think.

The stream widened as it went. Soon the trail disappeared and there was little but steep and slippery rock to climb over. It was not easy, but she pushed on, using her hands for balance and to hold on to the side of the ravine through which the stream was rushing.

It was a lonely place she was going to as she remembered it. The pond was a place of mystery, gray and green and deep. She recalled small outcroppings on the high stone walls where trees managed somehow to put down roots and cling as if by willpower.

She continued on for perhaps an hour. The steep cliffs opened at last and then the pond was before her. Far above, the rocks seemed to weep with dripping moisture, and moss hung like curtains. Near the water were ferns and the small stunted trees she remembered. Far above, there was a square of blue sky with white clouds that looked like small goats floating in the wind. Many years ago, White Hare had been brought here to observe a ceremony. The new initiates were being introduced to the commoners. There were always at least twelve antap in a village in addition to the alchuklash. Some villages had more, already trained to take over initiations and prayers during summer and winter solstice days and the harvest ceremony in case any of the first twelve became sick or died.

White Hare wondered why these who had training in sight and wisdom were not feeling the danger as strongly as she did. All of the forces and powers on the earth had to be kept in harmony. Everyone knew that. The Aztecs were creating conflict, fear and disorder. Forces had to be realigned or the world could crack open. Even White Hare knew that much. It seemed, from how the antap handled the threat, that she was the only one who knew.

She leaned against a huge boulder alongside the pond to rest and think. All she could see of the world from here were the rocks, the trees and the sky, but somehow, she did not feel alone. Then she looked out over the water. Boulders very much like the one she leaned on protruded from the surface of the pond, rough, gray and oddly shaped. Perhaps they were as ancient as the "shell rock" or even as old as the mountains themselves. It looked to White Hare like ancient monsters who prowled the first world before the Flood had suddenly turned to stone.

The boulders reflected perfectly upside down on the unmoving, polished surface of the water. She held a hand out over the pond and saw it again in the water. She crept up to the ledge and looked down, seeing her face exactly as unmoving as the stones. No ripples, no disturbances were here; only pure reflecting water.

Suddenly, she was eleven years old in the mouth of the cave where her grandfather had been brought to die. She was kneeling beside him and his thoughts were speaking in her mind.

"I will speak to you when you need me, White Hare, at the place of the reflecting water."

"Oh, Grandfather!" she cried from the depths of her being. "Now! I need you now! What can I do, Grandfather? The Aztecs are threatening us. They want to change us and make us into warriors to do their bidding. Tomorrow, they will begin to make us belong to their gods. They will sacrifice, they will kill my friends' babies. They will kill any of us who resist them. No one wants to die under the hooves of the horses. No one knows how to make them go away.

"Grandfather, the Antap are telling us we must compromise with them. I know we must not, but no one will listen to me. We will be slaves in our own land."

Anger filled her again, and denial, as if by her will she could turn back the forces herself.

She looked down into the water again. One girl, alone, looked back at her. With a small voice, plaintively, mournfully, she repeated, "What can I do?"

Her eyes were drawn to the reflection of one of the oddly shaped boulders. It looked a little like the back of a man, kneeling and covered with a hide robe. She could see where the elbows were under the robe, and the bowed head. It would be an old man, craggy, like the rocks. If he turned just a little, she could see him.

She felt a heaviness as if she were under water herself. Her eyelids became heavy and closed by themselves. She felt too ponderous to move, a living part of the rock behind her. A warm damp wind pushed her hair back.

"Open your eyes," Grandfather's voice said kindly. She could see him now, reflecting on the water, looking up into her astonished eyes. His face was wrinkled and knowing. "You are tall, my little White Hare. You're almost grown. You look strong and capable."

"Did you hear me, Grandfather? Do you know what is happening?"

"I know," he said. "I know that the priests do nothing and my granddaughter comes alone to the place of the priests. The gods want to help, but the People have to do their part. Child of Chupu, you are the only one. I knew you, at least, would come."

What was Grandfather saying? "I'm only one and one isn't enough. No one will listen to me. I don't know how to fight. I speak with no power." Somehow, it did not seem strange at all that she was arguing with a dream.

"You have more power than you know, child. Close your eyes and take your mind back to the day you saved the colt. Remember his cry. Recall it."

She obeyed. She heard the sound of the baby horse crying as he struggled, and the answering scream from his mother as she came running. The stallion was thundering after her and the other mares were drawing closer. She shook again with fright as they approached. She got the colt free of the twisted vines and was standing at his side, bent over his neck and unable to move. Her eyes were shut tight and she was waiting to be trampled for touching one of the forbidden horses.

She watched herself as a ghost watches. She heard the harsh voices of the warriors as they ran toward her. While the image of her trembled with fear, her eyes shut; her ghost self hovered close enough to see the truth.

The animals were not rearing to crush her as she imagined. They were touching her with their soft, warm muzzels as if they wanted to know her better and thank her for saving the baby.

The image she saw of herself only opened her eyes in time to see them turn fierce and angry, their eyes red and burning, because the warriors were pulling them by the ropes they threw around their necks and leading them back to their enclosure. The horses were not angry at her at all. Their hate was directed toward their masters! They were slaves to the foreigners because they feared them.

"The horses don't want to fight us, Grandfather," White Hare exclaimed, astonished as she realized this new truth.

"They won't have to if they are not there to fight. Will they, White Hare?"

Not there? What was Grandfather suggesting?

"If they wanted to go, they could have run when they were all loose, when the colt was in trouble."

"They needed guidance, child. They were afraid."

"You don't mean that I—" she could barely go on with the thought. "I can guide them?"

"You must go with them," Grandfather said. "The male is willing to carry you. The others will follow."

In her mind's eye, as she leaned in a semi-trance against the boulder, she saw herself leap up to the back of the stallion. He waited only until she had a secure grip on his neck before he danced away from the warriors. She felt a freedom and an exhilaration she could not believe. She held on with her knees and entangled her hands in his mane.

She leaned forward. "Away!" she screamed and they darted down the hill. No one could touch them. "Where are we to go, Grandfather?"

"You must take them toward the Big Valley. Then, east." His voice was the wind rushing past her ears in the darkness. "East." The word seemed to repeat over and over in the thudding of her heart. It seemed to her that she knew, or some part of her knew, where to go. She was almost flying. It was not possible to move this fast unless one was a bird soaring on the wind. Only in her datura vision did she move more swiftly.

"How long must I stay with them, Grandfather? I don't want to live away from my mountains."

"Only until they are sure of their freedom."

White Hare and the horses seemed to float above the

ground as they ran. Trees and chaparral parted as they bore down the hills and between the peaks. They flew over streams and narrow chasms, the arroyos.

There were villages along their path, but before the people could rush out to see them, they were far away. They passed beyond the land of the Chumash and then through the lands of the Shoshoni. They were heading toward the Great Valley, where the Tongva lived. Soon, below them would be the great Tongva village of Canoga, but the horses would not stop there. White Hare knew the green valley was bordered by arid and rocky mountains that led to the Great Desert. It was so wide that only a few—and those were experienced traders—had actually crossed it and come back. It was said that a few hardy tribes actually lived in the desert, people who subsisted on caterpillars, fly larvae, and lizards. Could the horses live there, or was it even farther that they must go?

"What will their land be like, Grandfather? What will they find there?"

Across a vast, empty space, the wind seemed to answer in her grandfather's voice, but very faintly. "Freedom to run and to grow numerous. Grassy plains to share with great beasts called buffalo, and people who will befriend them.

"More than three hundred summers will pass. Then a horde of white invaders like the ones who are destroying the great cities to the south will overrun the homes of the Plains People and try to take their land away from them. When that time comes, people of our blood, who have respect for the Mother, will have allies and companions; the descendants of these very horses."

"Will they drive the invaders away, Grandfather? Or will all the land and all the People's nations be destroyed and forgotten?"

"I do not know. It is too far in distance and time to see." She felt tears begin, both for the fate of those future People and because she could tell that he was leaving her again. She watched herself riding the stallion down a long slope toward the graying sky after a long night, but she felt the roughness of the boulder against her back, and the images were fading. She wondered if her grandfather would ever speak to her again before she joined the world of the spirits when she, too, died.

"What will be the names of the nations of the People?" she asked, hoping for an answer, for another moment with him. Whoever those people were, she envied them for having the horses. As they were in her vision, she had come to love them.

Only a ghost of a voice answered her. She could just hear the unfamiliar syllables. It said, "Comanche, Apache, Sioux," the names of people she would never know.

She was back. The reflection of the rock in the water, from a certain angle, looked like the back of an old man covered with a robe, but it was only a rock and she was alone again.

It was late in the afternoon before White Hare finally returned. Blue Star sat in front of the small house working on a basket. Her mother looked up at her, but she did not say anything. White Hare had a wild look about her eyes as if they saw things others did not. Her hair, which was usually neatly braided or hanging long and loose and silky, flew around her face in tangles as if she was standing in a strong wind. She was scratched and bruised, but she seemed not to notice.

The younger and the older woman regarded each other steadily. At last, Blue Star broke the silence. "I brought food home for you. I hoped you would come back to us."

"Thank you," White Hare said simply. She went into the dim hut and found a wooden bowl of acorn mush covered with leaves. She brought it outside into the sunlight, sat down and scooped up the food with two fingers. When she finished, she went down to the stream to wash the bowl. She splashed water all over herself as well to wash away the worst of the grime and to clean her scratches. In a little while she came back and sat next to Blue Star, wondering how to heal the wound between them. It was more than a scratch.

"I was worried," Blue Star said, as if she was talking to herself. White Hare knew she did not have to respond if she did not wish to speak. Mother was trying to make peace between them. It came to White Hare that she was an adult too. Mother had made the first move. Whatever their disagreement, she loved her mother and perhaps she was being less than fair.

"There was no need for you to worry, Mother." White Hare spoke with a new sound in her voice. The passion and the youthful exuberance were gone. In their place was a serenity and a surety that were not there before. "I was with Grandfather."

Blue Star gasped. Her daughter was grown now and did not have to account for how she spent her time. She could say what she wished or say nothing, but to speak of her grandfather? Blue Star did not know what to think. It was not like White Hare to make things up. Wherever she had gone, it was inconceivable that she would do anything that harmful to the village; but to speak now of Blue Star's father, now, when the whole village was in a turmoil—if only he were here now to advise them!

"Mother. I have to go away. I'm not sure how long I'll be gone. I came back to tell you and Father, so you wouldn't worry."

This was not what Blue Star expected to hear. She knew White Hare was upset. They all were upset, Black Raven with the antap and Gray Eagle with those who wanted to fight were at odds. The village was breaking into two opposing camps. Was the problem one to be dealt with by the alchuklash and the antap priests with compromise or by the wot and the men in battle? War was physical. New gods to consider was an antap matter. The People must not be divided. Had anyone even thought to ask the spirits for guidance? All these thoughts flashed through Blue Star's mind in an instant.

Suddenly, it all came together. Her father spoke to White Hare. Her father wanted to help and White Hare was the only one he could speak with. The tension between mother and daughter evaporated like dew under the hot summer sun as Blue Star understood the truth.

"Is there anything we can do to help?"

"Pray for me. Mother, I'm frightened." Blue Star pulled White Hare closer and threw her arms around her as if she could protect her with her body from whatever harm might come to her.

"I will. Of course I will," she said strongly. "So will Father."

Escape

White Hare slept for several hours. When she awoke, her father was standing over her. She stood up and walked into his outstretched arms. He embraced her. Then he went to a high shelf to get something. "Take this," he said, handing her a small leather pouch. She felt the pine nuts through the bag. She tied it to her belt. She could not carry much, but it was said a traveler could live for a day on a small amount of these sweet seeds from the northern forests. She had never expected the chance to find out if it was true.

She told no one except her parents anything of what she planned to do. Her dream was not a prophecy and she had no guarantee that the dream and reality would be the same. Would the stallion allow her to mount him? How could she make the horses come to her and away from the warriors who guarded them so closely? Could she find paths the animals could manage through the mountains and the chaparral with only the stars and the moon to light the way? She might be killed before she even left the mountain. She only knew that she had to try.

She ate again before sunset. Her mother brought her food again and she ate within the keesh. Seeing her friends and hearing the frightened discussions of the villagers might scatter her thoughts just when she needed most of all to keep them resolute. Later, she emptied the water from her body. She needed nourishment for strength; she needed to be free from discomfort. All she could do was to rely on her feelings to tell her the right things to do to embark on her trial correctly. She had to endeavor to gain knowledge from her innermost feelings. She had no more idea about how to mount or guide a horse than what she observed and what she felt in her dream. If the horse did not choose to cooperate, she was lost.

Tomorrow was the day the Aztecs planned the make their sacrifice. White Hare imagined Mara tied and left in a corner of the tent like a sheaf of willow branches. With luck, the other women were getting food to her. Without luck, she would die tomorrow, and she would not be the only one.

The moon rose at last over the mountains. White Hare waited in her usual watching place, her chin cupped on her joined hands. She was fairly certain she could not be seen by her enemies. If any of her own saw her, well, they had seen her before during her vigils. In any case, tonight, she was not the only one watching.

She waited until all the horses were in the corral and only the two guards were near them. One by one, the small fires in the village and at the camp were extinguished. She felt a strength in herself that was a part of her determination and it gave her a clarity of purpose and vision. She felt as poised for action as a bobcat awaiting the exact moment to pounce on her prey.

While she waited, she considered that it was usually the females in the animal world that were the fiercest. They were the ones that hunted and defended their families. Among humans, the tasks were shared. From what she had overheard, she knew the Chumash were superior to the Aztecs in their family and village loyalties. The men who threatened her village were bullies and not only bullies, but cowards. For them to behave like peacocks, showing off and being so arrogant, for them to even imagine that women were only for work and childbearing showed how much less than animals the southerners really were.

Mara and the other women did not come from the same land as Toacoatl and his men. Mara understood more about loyalty than these examples of the Aztec nation. If the rest of them were as cruel and cowardly as these few, she hardly felt sorry for them. Perhaps there were those among them that were kind and just. Whoever was invading their land was probably just as bad or even worse. The outcome of Aztec struggle against their enemies was in the hands of fate.

The evening began to grow cool, but still White Hare waited. Everyone but the two guards seemed to have finally retired for the night. The guards finished their rounds and sat, one leaning against the tent and the other against the fence of the corral. It was very late. An owl hooted nearby. Bats made whirring noises as they flew among the trees in search of lizards and small rodents. Far away and very faintly, a pair of coyotes took turns howling at the moon.

White Hare went very quietly down the trial and positioned herself on the path that led to Satwiwa. The mountains were crisscrossed with trails. From there, she hoped she would be able to find trails that avoided the worst of the terrain and that would be broad enough for the horses to manage. She also hoped that their passage in the night would not awaken her cousins.

She stopped when her village was still in sight up on the hill. A call could be heard at the camp from here. Then she closed her eyes and brought back the memory of the colt's struggle. He was lost, scared to be away from his mother. He had not been badly hurt when he fell among the vines, but he could not free himself. His cry had been more from fear than from physical pain, and it had increased when he saw someone running toward him. It was White Hare, of course, only wanting to help, but it frightened him even more until he felt her arms around him, soothing and comforting him. He must have felt, with the memory of his species, that he was about to become victim to a predator. A baby antelope will freeze in fear when it cannot run; it must be the instinct of a horse to scream for help.

She imagined herself in the mind of the horse child now, trapped and feeling itself stalked by a mountain lion. She wanted to run, to put distance between herself and her attacker, but she could not. If she was cornered, she would want to kick with her hooves at the one who threatened her. But what if she was trapped, tangled up in vines and unable to move? In her mind she saw a figure running toward her out of the shadows. She imagined it crouching low, getting ready to spring, its white, sharp fangs glistening. She felt the pure terror felt by the colt. Mother was near somewhere. Father was close. Call for help. Put all your strength and terror into one desperate call.

She was the colt and her cry filled the air. It pierced. It broke the silence of the night and shattered it. (She was seeing the world through the large eyes of an animal for the moment. It was not like in her datura vision, when she was White Hare within the mind of another creature.) In her mind for a moment, she *was* the colt.

Answering screams filled the night. The stallion reared and pounded with his hooves on the gate of the corral. The mares cried and lent their weight to the effort. One of their babies was out there, threatened and afraid. They had to go.

The Aztec warriors were like flies to be flicked off when a child was in danger. The gate fell flat, pushed down by eight mighty hooves. The three colts followed and all the horses were away and galloping down the hill toward the path where White Hare waited.

The stallion was first to reach her, his eyes on fire, looking for a colt and an enemy to fight. White Hare got out of her crouch and reached for him. He leaned down and smelled her hair. Then he snorted, pawing the ground impatiently, questioning. Where was the colt?

"Father," she said, still half in her self-induced vision. "Will you carry me?" He let her touch him, bending his strong head down to her. He knew her now. In a moment, she was herself again. "Let me bring you to a place of freedom. Let me," she begged.

The three mares and the colts were with her now, too, stamping their feet. Warriors from the encampment were close behind them. The men were screaming their war cries.

The stallion knelt. She got astride him and he stood just as the Aztecs were closing in. "Go!" she screamed. "Take us away!" She held on to him tightly, her knees clasped to his sides, her hands in his mane as he leaped forward. The mares kicked and fought any who tried to get near the colts. Several of the soldiers were on the ground nursing wounds as White Hare and the horses disappeared down the hill and out of sight.

A new war cry sounded on the mountain, one that had not been heard for generations, as the men of Simo'mo rushed onto the scene. Dancing Bear was first among the younger men. As soon as they arrived, they put arrows to their bows and took aim at their enemies. The older men were right behind them, many of them carrying spears or knives. Goat Killer was just in time to see what his daughter did. No father could have been prouder.

Gray Eagle ran to the fore. Black Raven and the antap were with him and behind them were the women. The Aztec warriors got to their feet. They stood like statues. It was as if they could not believe what their eyes told them.

Gray Eagle spoke. "It seems that your power has been taken out of your hands." When the foreigners did not reply, he continued.

"Your actions and demands are beyond tolerance. You may take what you can carry and leave now. If you are still here by morning, even gentle Chupu, Mother of us all, might develop a taste for blood."

The Aztec men ran to their tent. Without the horses to do the carrying, they began to pile the skins and the tent poles and the food pouches on the backs of the women.

"Wait!" Blue Star's voice called loudly. "Mara, Sena, Rasha! Do you want to go back with these men?"

Mara, unbound, dropped her burdens. "Will you give us a home?" She spoke for all the women.

Blue Star shouted, "Gray Eagle, Black Raven—may they stay here?"

The civil chief and the spiritual chief consulted briefly. Then Gray Eagle turned back. "I grant the women sanctuary," he said with great authority. "Toacoatl, you and your men have tried our patience for the last time. You will take your men and your things and leave now, or you will be so filled with arrows you will look like cactus. None of your kind will ever be allowed in Chumash country again."

The last the villagers saw of the Aztecs were their backs, piled up with their gear. They were tripping and running in fear down the steep path that led down to the shore. Gray Eagle decided to send runners that very night to warn the other towns and villagers not to give them a welcome in any of the Chumash lands.

So quickly it was over. The villagers were safe, sleeping in their houses now that the threat was gone. The corral was torn down. Tomorrow was soon enough to break it up for firewood. It was almost as if the Aztec threat had never been, except for the prayers of two

parents sitting quietly in their keesh, floating up to the
Mother to keep their daughter safe and return her unharmed to them.

Return

One young man remained standing in the path below the village long after everyone else was gone. How wrong he had been—what a fool! Now White Hare was alone somewhere out there. By this time, even if he had a horse of his own, she must be so far away, he could never catch up. He could not find her; he could not help her. What if she were frightened or lost or hurt? There was only one thing he knew he could do. It was a risk he would not be prepared to take for anyone else.

At first, he walked aimlessly among the rocks, not finding what he was seeking. Then, he turned his eyes up to the constellations. "Help me, Sky Coyote," he pleaded. He waited, listening. Soon, he heard the howl a coyote makes when the moon is full. He followed the sound.

When he found it, he was far from the village. There was the white cup-shaped flower, the deep green leaves, deeper even by moonlight than the plants that grew around it. Nearby stood a young tree. He broke off a branch of it and dug out the whole plant, carrying it back to the stream, where he washed it thoroughly. There was no time to prepare it properly, even if he knew how, and there was no priest to guard him. He knew the risk. Only the thought that White Hare was possibly in danger with no one to help spurred him to act in a way that was completely contrary to caution.

He knew there was a small cave downstream at the foot of a rock cliff. Here, he might be safe from the predators that prowled at night. In a datura trance, he would be no more capable of defending himself or fighting than a dead man. With a final prayer, he put the root to his mouth and began to chew.

Far away in the night, White Hare continued her ride. The horses were finding their own way now. She was too exhausted to do more than hang on. From time to time, the horses stopped to rest and look around. The stallion's breath came in small clouds from his nostrils as he turned to check that his family was keeping up.

In her dream, she and the animals had floated. In reality, she was jolted and jarred. Her muscles were aching from holding on. Her legs were getting scratched by the chaparral. The animals had to pick their way through where some of the seldom-used trail was overgrown again by the encroaching bushes. Through the night, no matter how the trails meandered to avoid the steep grade of the mountains, they continued to head northeast.

Finally, White Hare found a way to be more comfortable. The stallion steadied to an easy lope on a clear part of the trail. Her arms were loosening from around his neck and her legs were too tired to hold on so tightly. She brought them up so that she was almost reclining as she rested on his broad back. The rhythm of the seven running horses reminded her of the pounding of the surf as the waves crashed into the rocks on the shore.

Her eyelids began to feel warm and heavy and she was almost asleep when the stallion increased his pace to a full gallop. The change in his stride shook her wide awake. She saw in front of them, in startling clarity, the black crack of a narrow arroyo. The young ones slowed to find a way around it, but the adults saw it in time to speed up to cross it in a flying leap.

White Hare tried to get herself into a position where she might have a better hold, but she could not move quickly enough. It was all she could do to keep from falling as the stallion gathered his muscles for the effort. She felt herself start to slip as he took off. She was suspended over nothing. Before she could scream, a strong wind seemed to push her back and hold her steady. They were on the other side.

When White Hare opened her eyes at long last, she saw before them a huge panorama framed by mountains under the suffused light of the predawn sun. White Hare had not even noticed when the young ones had joined them again.

The stars were beginning to dim and the sky was gray now. The night was almost over. White Hare's dream took her only as far as a valley so large that one could barely see the eastern mountains. She knew this was where the Tongva nation had their homes; beyond the great and rocky mountains to the north and the east was the Great Desert. The time had come for parting.

She dismounted. Her legs almost collapsed under her as she tried to stand, she felt so weak. She held on to the stallion's mane and rested her head on his shoulder. The mares and the young ones came close to touch her with their warm muzzles and their soft lips. They all seemed content to rest for a little while.

It seemed to White Hare that just before morning was the time when the spirits and the ghosts of the departed were closest to the living. Often this was just the time that souls chose to depart their bodies, when those of their friends and relatives who had gone first were waiting nearby to show them the path into eternity. The Mistress of Life would surely be listening now. White Hare picked her words carefully.

"Dear Mother of the Earth," she began, "Mother of the mountains and the deserts and the valleys and all things, Chupu. Grandfather called me your child. I don't understand why he said it like that because we are all your children; but I beg you, not for me, but for the People, please watch over this family of horses, the father and his three wives and their children. Keep them from harm. Tell the sun, who watches everything from his crystal house, not to burn them. Help them to find enough water in the places where they will go. Help them to find enough food and show them the way to the people they are destined for.

"Please help them, Earth Mother. I know I'm still young and I don't know very much about your mysteries. I don't ask to be important. I don't even ask to be a wisewoman like my mother unless it is your wish and if I show that I am worthy. I only ask to be permitted to live in peace in the land of my people. I want to be able to visit the sea and the land to harvest what you give us for our needs. I want my children and my grandchildren to be able to live in peace in our own land. And—and please let the father of my children be Dancing Bear. I know he would help me raise them to respect and love you too. I wish I could tell Dancing Bear what I feel. I lose my courage to speak to him when he's near me, but you know that, don't you?" She said this last hesitantly, looking down at the ground, embarrassed to say these words aloud to the Earth Mother, who probably knew her mind better than she did herself.

She felt warm all over as she came to the end of her prayer. She had not really intended to ask a favor for herself. But there it was; again, she had spoken before she thought. Scarlet streaks in the eastern sky were announcing the sun. Confident now that Chupu would help them find their new home, she took her hands from the stallion's mane. He no longer needed the guidance of a young Chumash girl.

"Earth Mother will guide you now," she told him. "Trust her, but remember also to be strong and to keep your family together. Watch out for dangers." She pulled his head down to her and touched her cheek to his long face. "Remember, go to the east, to the land where the sun rises, until you find your home. I'm sure you'll know it when you get there." He whinnied into her hair gently and blew warm air through his nose.

White Hare put her arms around the three colts and then caressed the faces of the mares. "Chupu be with you. Now, go swiftly." She gave them a little push to start them on their way.

The horses began to walk; slowly at first. Then, they picked up speed as they ran down the hill. At the top of the next rise, they stopped and turned back. She lifted her arm in a final wave. She knew she would never see them again. They began the descent and were gone.

Her feelings were mixed. She felt a sharp pang of sadness at their loss, but she was also relieved. They were not meant to stay with her; the fates had other plans for them. They had never really been hers at all, she told herself a little sharply. Well, maybe they had been, but only for one night. She could never conceive of owning them or thinking of them as property. Horses were not meant to be owned any more than people were. They had been her friends, if only for a brief time, and she must be glad for them that they were free.

She turned back and felt panic for just a moment as she faced the unfamiliar mountains. She had never been so far away from home as this. "Oh, Chupu, please, help me get home too," she begged. Then she had to chuckle at the simplicity of this little prayer after her long words on behalf of the horses.

The path seemed to radiate a golden light for her to follow as the sun grew higher over the mountains. It was far to travel on foot all those miles she had traveled with her friend, the stallion, beneath her, but she was sure now that Chupu was not too busy to watch over her also and that she would find her way back. A hawk flew overhead, calling to his mate and welcoming the day.

She had only the small sack of pine nuts that her father had given her for food. She drank at springs and streams, always finding one when her thirst became too great. She supplemented this with berries when she could find them and the tender leaves of several plants she knew to be safe. She plopped a few pine nuts into her mouth every now and then. She knew she might stop and dig for roots. There were many that she could eat even without stopping to make a fire to roast them, but she wanted to get home.

Even White Hare's strong, young legs could not carry her in one day back as far as she came with the horses through the night. She stopped to rest at the end of the day in the tall grass near a tree, with nothing over her but the stars. She was very weary, and she slept before the moon rose.

It was almost daybreak again when Dancing Bear found her under the tree, fast asleep. He grinned to see how she was curled up with her arm under her head, looking almost, but not quite, like a child. Before he covered her with his rabbit fur robe, he saw that there were many scratches on her arms and legs and that her feet were black. She had traveled very far but still had most of a day yet to walk.

At least for the rest of the way he would be with her. He had been with her before, of course, during the night, but only in spirit. It was so much easier to help when you were in your body, Dancing Bear thought happily.

It was easier, when one was in one's body, to caress also. It was something he wished to do ever since he had heard her prayer. No. It was a thing he had wished he could do ever since when they were twelve she had told him they were too young for love. He had waited for her ever since. If only he could find the words it would take to convince her.

He would not disturb her rest. She had earned it. Asking for courage, indeed. After what she risked to save her people, who had more?

As the morning approached, the birds began their songs. She opened her eyes and saw him standing over her. "Dancing Bear?" she asked softly. She was almost sure she was awake, but it did not make sense for him to be here watching her sleep when she was still a day's journey from home. She stretched and as she did, she felt his robe covering her and keeping her warm. This was not part of a dream. "You found me. How did you know where to look?"

"I knew. Sky Coyote showed me where you would stop in my trance."

She understood at once. "You took datura out of season with no priest to guard your soul. You were out of your body. You might have died!" she cried out, instantly ashamed at showing her fear for him.

"You might have died yourself if I wasn't with you to keep you from falling when the horse jumped over the arroyo, so it was worth the risk. Do you think I want to lose you, now that I finally know how you feel about me?"

She felt hot all over. Her face was warm and it was not even under the robe. She realized her mouth was still open. She closed it, but she was not yet able to respond. He was with her!

He told her what had happened after she left the village, to save her from having to speak. "Our people drove away the warriors, Toacoatl with them. No one was killed even though were were ready to fight if they resisted. The village is at peace again. The Aztecs were cowards. They ran from us. Perhaps they went back where they came from. I don't think they'll give us trouble again." She was still unable to speak.

"So you didn't care for Toacoatl after all?" Dancing Bear asked with half a smile. "I thought you did. I thought that was why you visited him in his tent. I thought you liked him ever since he arrived. That's why I stayed away. I thought you wanted a warrior for your husband."

He was jealous! That accounted for the strain and the confusion between them. She had feared that he did not like her at all. He thought she actually wanted Toacoatl for her husband. If only she had not been shy.

"You know now I did not," she answered at last. It hardly seemed possible. Her prayer had been answered the moment she uttered it.

"What happened to the women?" White Hare wanted to know, but she asked now, to avoid the special words she wanted to say and hear. It was all happening too fast and she needed to compose herself.

"The women will stay with us in the village. Their men lost their courage when they lost their horses and the women finally stood up to them. Your mother asked Gray Eagle and Black Raven to allow them to stay. The wot and the alchuklash are at peace again. Families from the village will adopt Mara and Sena and Rasha. As soon as they're ready, the priests will find them husbands who will cherish them instead of masters who will use them. I think they'll finally be happy."

White Hare stood up, gathering the robe around her. It moved gently in the morning breeze. She did not want to ask her question from the ground. She stood face to face with Dancing Bear, her eyes almost level with his. "And I? Will I be happy too?"

He put his hand on her shoulder tenderly and drew her closer. "I have been thinking about that." He smiled as he pushed the hair away from her eyes. "Would you like the name 'Horse Freer' for your married name? Everyone would know of your courage and honor you for it."

White Hare smiled back to him slowly, radiantly, her eyes glittering. "As long as you do. That's all that really matters." They embraced at last, standing under the oak tree with no one to see but the birds and the mountains and Chupu.

"Let's go home," she said.

Author's Note

This is, of course, a fictional story. But the places I described are real. They are all there, in the Santa Monica Mountains. I began to walk the hiking trails through the Santa Monicas almost three years ago and I have stood at Satwiwa and seen the hills over the plains at Simo'mo. It is about four miles inland from Point Mugu. Point Mugu Rock stands near Muwu, the southern Chumash capital. Near it, at La Jolla Canyon, still lies the Old Chumash Trail on which the young people from the village of Simo'mo walked carrying their baskets of fish and shell food from the Pacific Ocean to their home.

The pond of the reflecting waters is Rock Pond. The rock formations, stone cliffs, and still water are so picturesque that several film studios chose this very spot for the location filming of a number of movies. It was formed by Malibu Creek and is really closer to the Chumash village of Talopop than to Simo'mo, but it can be visited. Streams and ponds were often the scenes of extraordinary happenings in Chumash mythology and legend.

Chumash land extended from Topanga Canyon in the south past Santa Barbara, which was called Syuxtun then and was their northern capital, for about another two hundred miles. Because of their peacefulness, their story and their culture are largely underrated or ignored.

They were great astronomers, lived under laws, had currency, government, manufacturing and trade. Their plank canoes, tomols, were the finest vessels made in the Americas. Their trading caravans went far beyond their own borders into Mexico and Arizona and as far North as Oregon.

This book takes place in the early 1520s, when the European invasion had only just begun. I would like to think that Horse Freer, the White Hare of the story, lived happily for many years in her beloved mountains. I would like to believe that she and her husband, Great Bear, the former Dancing Bear, had many children and grandchildren. It was not until August of 1769 that Gaspar de Portola came up from Mexico through the Sepulveda Pass, crossed the Great Valley (now called the San Fernando Valley) and followed the Santa Clara River to the coast. He gave the mountains, the valley and the river the names they bear today.

Before Portola came, the great Spanish ships sailed by the Santa Monica Mountains on their trading voyages to the Philippines. Horse Freer and Great Bear's children and grandchildren could have seen them, but if any Spanish sailors came ashore, the Chumash would have hidden themselves.

I believe they would have known from rumors of them coming up out of the south that the Spaniards came to the lands of the People always bearing gifts of cloth and beads and speaking soft words about a new god. In the south, many had been coerced into giving up their ancestral gods for new ones and their old ways for new ways.

As I imagine Horse Freer would have predicted, foreigners finally arrived on horses. The foreigners made promises to the Chumash. Her warning had been left on stone. A painting of four horsemen is still visible in a cave in the southern Santa Monica Mountains to remind the People of the time four horsemen came up from the south and threatened Horse Freer's village. The danger had then been averted by the bravery of a fifteen-year-old girl.

"If horsemen come," she would have told her people, "don't go with them. Make them go away. Their promises will ensnare you. Never forsake our Mother, the Earth, for a false god. Never leave our mountains."

Unfortunately, after Horse Freer died, the People forgot her warning. The Spanish missions were built during the last decades of the eighteenth century by the first of the "Indian" converts the Spanish were able to get under their control. The great *ranchos* were built and fenced. To get the Chumash and the Tongva and the others out of the way, the tribes were "invited" to leave their homes and to come live at the missions.

Missionaries did make promises about the benefits of a new way of life and a new religion. The antap usually went first. They felt it was their duty to protect their people by trying to understand the new forces that were coming into their land. They had to investigate and see how they might form compromises so that peace would be maintained. A new power needed study. The Spanish soldiers and priests certainly had power as could readily be seen by their great ships, their cloth and their horses.

Most of the common people followed, willingly at first. When they realized their mistake, it was, tragically, too late. Those who tried to leave to go home were often shot. Disobedience was punished by beatings. To be caught worshipping the old gods was a crime and a heresy of these new converts, who did not know they were being enslaved when men in black sprinkled water on their heads.

Antap were burned at the stake as an example to others not to go back to their own gods. After their forced conversions, their souls belonged to the Catholic church and their bodies to the king of Spain as represented by his soldiers and governors.

Until the last of the antap priests and priestesses died, they led the People in secret ceremonies to Chupu, the Earth Mother. The rites were kept secret so well that they are now gone from memory. Most of the Chumash who were forced to live in the missions died in epidemics of smallpox and tuberculosis, or from cruel treatment and longing for their homes.

Chumash are still living among us in Southern California. Many of them are again looking for their roots and working toward the building of a cultural center where they can relearn their own history, and where those who are interested in the people who lived here before the great invasions can learn about them and their culture and life-style.

If you are interested in the Chumash and their cultural center, please write to Friends of Satwiwa, 4126 Potrero Road, Newbury Park, California 91320. The center will stand on the site of the old Chumash village of Satwiwa. Charlie Cooke, hereditary chief of the southern Chumash, is president of the Friends.

I have not seen the cave of the Four Horseman myself as I hope to do someday. It is one of the sacred places of the Chumash, but I have seen a photograph of the wall of the cave. It has been suggested that this must have been the Chumash perspective of Portola and his expedition. After the last Ice Age there were no horses in the Americas until the Spaniards brought them in the 1500s, yet within a short time they were already populating the Plains. Since the riders in the cave painting looked to me as if they were wearing feathers, my story is an alternative suggestion. In Christian mythology four horsemen are a portent of doom. It is interesting to note that pre-Christian "Indians" painted the picture.